OX UNDER PRESSURE

John Ney
OX UNDER PRESSURE

J

J. B. LIPPINCOTT COMPANY
PHILADELPHIA AND NEW YORK

U.S. LIBRARY OF CONGRESS CATALOGING IN PUBLICATION DATA

NEY, JOHN, BIRTH DATE
    OX UNDER PRESSURE.

    SUMMARY: WHEN HE ACCOMPANIES HIS FATHER TO LONG ISLAND, SEVEN-
TEEN-YEAR-OLD OX IS UNPREPARED FOR THE BITTERSWEET EXPERIENCES THAT
FOLLOW HIS MEETING WITH AN UNUSUAL GIRL.
    I.   TITLE.
PZ7.N4878OZ   [FIC]   75-38752
ISBN-0-397-31653-4

FOR _____, WHO TEASED

OX UNDER PRESSURE

1

IN THE FIRST STORIES I told about myself, I explained how I'd had to go on a long chase to find out what a cow looked like, and how I'd had to go to camp in Vermont. That wasn't all that happened on those trips—just the way they started. Plenty happened after that, more than I'd want to start going into now. And maybe you've already read those stories and know all about what went on.

Especially that each time it started with some idea of Dad's. It was his idea to show me what a cow looked like—and we ended up going all over this country and Mexico to find one. And it was his idea to send me to camp, and that ended in a mess, too. Every time he has an idea for me, it just doesn't work out. And this time was no exception. It was his idea to go to . . . but I'm getting ahead of myself.

The trouble with telling more than one story about yourself is that you never know from one to the next how much to put in that was explained before. I mean, in the first one I told about myself and my family in Palm Beach. In the second one I figured I didn't have to do that again. But then I wondered about the people who hadn't read the first one—how were they going to pick all that up in the second one if I skipped it? So I sort of compromised—I told a little bit, and then got going.

This time I'm going to cut it closer. Outside of saying that I'm seventeen now and bigger than ever, I'm not going to go into anything. I'll say plenty as I go along, but nothing more now.

Dad's changed a lot in the last two years. He always did talk in a sarcastic, no-hope way, but he acted another way. I mean, he still had his safaris and parties and general pleasures. His liver gave him a bad time for a while, but he got it back under control and says he'll never lose another round to it, whatever that means. Mom . . . well, I always say Mom is always the same, and she always is. As long as the money holds out and there are parties, Mom is going to be the same.

Terry and Beth, my sisters, aren't around much anymore. Terry got married to the grandson of some sportsman and they live in Pittsburgh and Tahiti. Beth goes to boarding school somewhere in the East. She's the only member of the family who's ever been able to stick it in school.

"I'm proud of her," Dad said to me one day. The two of us were having iced tea near the pool.

"You should be," I said. Like always, I agreed with him.

"You should be, too," he said.

"I am."

"You don't sound it."

"But I am, I really am."

"She's a great girl."

"That's right."

We drank tea without saying anything for a while, and then he said, "Ox, I've been thinking about morality."

I could have said it was a little late, but I wasn't that dumb. He was leaning forward in his chair, with his eyes fixed right on mine. I was thinking that he still looked good . . . if you didn't look too close. A solid tan, good teeth, body in pretty fair shape, all his hair, and he could still charm people when he wanted to. He didn't look exactly like a movie star, but he wasn't all that different, either, something about the way he came into a place like it was put there for him alone. Not one of the new stars, of course. You'd have to go back for Dad— back to the ones you only see on the old TV movies. The only halfway modern one he looks like is Bill Holden. Not exactly, the all-American part is missing, but there's a little bit there. Especially when he's being serious.

Anyhow, he was thinking about morality and leaning across the table at me with his eyes bulging a little.

"Do you know what morality is?" he asked me, man to man.

"Sure," I said, "the difference between right and wrong."

"That's a crude way to put it," he said, "but it'll pass. Ox, my problem is that my old values aren't doing it for me anymore."

It wasn't the first or the last time he said that. What he means is that he can't go on being a sportsman and

11

nothing else. He's been rich all his life, and just a natural playboy. Personally, I don't see what's so bad about that. Neither did he until a couple of years ago.

"I want to open my horizons," he was saying. "I need to grow."

He looked at me hard and I said, "That sounds good."

"It does not," he said. "It sounds lousy. The worst thing about it, though, is that it's true. Do you realize that until two years ago I'd never read a book? If you don't count mysteries? I was uncultured. Or worse."

He looked at the backs of his hands, but didn't explain what the worse was.

"They say a lot of people are," I said. "Uncultured, I mean. But does it always have to be so bad? If you . . ."

"Speak for yourself," he said sarcastically. Then he looked away, across the pool to the ocean, gearing himself for some real emotion. "I don't want to be a cultural dwarf all my life," he finally got out.

"I thought you were cultured just right," I said. "For what you want to do with it, I mean."

He swiveled around and looked at me hard again, but there was confusion there, too, so I babbled along. "If you get too cultured, you won't be able to do all the fun things you like. You'll be in an ivory tower, reading books, getting pale. You won't be the real Barry Olmstead at all. You really will be a cultural dwarf—a little guy with all the knowledge in the world riding on his shoulders. The kind that can speak fifteen languages and is ashamed he doesn't know sixteen . . ."

He waved his hand impatiently and I stopped. "Ox," he said, "you're wild. Usually you don't talk at all, and

12

then you suddenly open your mouth and let go. That wouldn't be bad, and I wouldn't even care if it was straight con, except . . . none of it makes sense. And sense is what I need now. I need sense, and what do I get?"

He looked up at the sky as if he was asking it the question, but that Palm Beach sky wouldn't answer anyone if it could.

"I was only trying to help," I said.

"I know," he said. "It's not your fault that you can't."

Then he was tired of it and started examining the backs of his hands again, and I could get away.

That's the way it always is with Dad and me. He talks at me and I pick it up and push it back somehow, and then he wonders how he got a son like me and I escape. I guess that happens between a lot of fathers and sons. I'm not good at figuring things out, but if I had to try, I'd say it comes down to Dad being a phony and me being a coward. Some kids (and a lot of adults) would say, "Well, what if he is a phony? That doesn't mean you should be phony back." But they're wrong, at least in Dad's case. If you're honest with him in any way, he turns into a killer. I know. And there's always the money angle, too. Most people—even the smart ones—don't know how different a rich phony is from a poor one. A poor phony can only go so far, but a rich one can play games you never dreamed of.

The other thing that's different about Dad and me is that neither one of us cares. When a poor father is a phony and treats everyone around him in a bad way because of that, it always turns out that he himself hates what he's doing, or something like that. He has a conscience, and it finally catches up with him and he either stops being a phony or drifts away and becomes a drunk or a suicide. But Dad has no conscience—if he had one, he couldn't be rich. He can do it forever and he couldn't care less. It works for him. It has to, because it's the whole system. Everyone in America wants to be rich, but not everyone can pay the price, of not caring. So it's not as crowded at the top as it might be. And if you want to stay there, you'd better remember not to care. About anything, including yourself.

When you get to the kids, the difference between me and a poor kid is a little like the difference between Dad and a poor father. Poor kids *care*. If their fathers are mean to them, they bite their lips and go out and talk to someone about it—a pal, or some nice old man, or even their dog. They go up and down with it, it's their whole life. Even if they hide it, some psychiatrist can go in there and find it and pin it on them. And all the time, they're supposed to be brave because they're putting up with it.

Rich kids can't afford all that. It's moving so much faster for them. They have to get with it and forget the problem or they're all washed up. Rich parents would get rid of them fast if they moaned around.

So I'm a coward. I admit it, but if I weren't I'd be dead or locked up. That's what happens to the few rich kids who are brave. I'm a coward because I want to live a little before I go.

If you're rich, you learn to pay no attention to what are supposed to be your troubles. Of course, rich kids are probably even more shot underneath. But they don't show it. They can't.

That's what I mean when I say that neither Dad nor I care. We just fence with each other and then walk away and forget it. He's not a father and I'm not a kid. Sounds hard, but it's probably easier in some ways.

And there's a cat-and-mouse side to it that makes it sort of interesting. I don't mean the game with Dad, but with myself. Most rich kids play the survival game, and that's all. I look like that's all I play—and maybe it is all I play—but sometimes I have other feelings. I don't mean mushy feelings like wanting a real dad and a real mom—they wouldn't do me any good now, anyhow—and I don't mean hard feelings, like revenge and meanness. I mean feelings that are hard to describe. As though there might be a way where you could slip through, where you'd feel right inside yourself, where you'd be yourself and never be ashamed to look yourself in the eye. It's a dream, but I try to keep it alive. No matter what happens, I try not to let myself go completely to pieces.

The only reason I go into all this heavy stuff is that if I didn't, you wouldn't understand a lot of what happened. Not only to me, but . . . well, to someone else, too. To a lot of people, in fact. So I have to explain myself a little. From the outside I just look like any other oversized rich kid trying to get by—except I'm more oversized than most—and that's ninety-nine percent of what I am. But with that last one percent I'm trying to keep my little candle from blowing out forever.

The hardest thing to explain is that it's not grim at all. It's sort of fun, or I wouldn't do it. I guess that's part of being rich, too—you have a better time because you expect so much less. Even Dad would agree with that.

But there are still things that . . . but I can't talk about them. I've said as much as I can. From now on, I can tell it, but I can't talk about it.

After I got away from Dad that day I went back into the house and was starting upstairs when Mom called me.

I went into the sitting room where she was and waited to hear what she wanted.

"I have a question for you," she said. "Sit down."

The room was filled with tropical plants and furniture in bright colors, a typical Palm Beach room. Sally Bracken, a friend of Mom's, was there with her and they were both in shorts and having an early drink. They both looked pretty good, in a way. I mean, they had good figures and they were brown and all that. In another way, they didn't look so good. Their eyes and the way their arms moved and things like that.

I sat down, but I didn't say hello to Sally Bracken. There's never a lot of point in using good manners in Palm Beach. You might win once in a while, but most of the time you just draw attention to yourself and get into trouble.

"I'm worried about Barry," Mom said to Sally Bracken, who nodded as if that was pretty close to what she expected.

"I saw you talking to him," Mom said to me. "What was he telling you?"

"What are you worried about?" I asked her.

"Just answer the question without the backtalk!" she flared up. Even in her set she's not considered smooth.

"That wasn't backtalk," I said.

"What's he up to?" she asked me.

"Thinking about his golf clubs or something," I said. I wasn't going to get in between them.

"He wouldn't talk to you about golf clubs," she said. "Ox is so unathletic," she explained to Sally.

"He looks big enough," Sally said.

"Size isn't everything," I said.

"It can go a long way," Sally said. She'd had more than one, I figured, and thought I was older than I was.

"Not all the way, though," I said.

"Cut it out," Mom said. She'd picked up Sally's confusion, too, and didn't think it was funny, the way I did. "Listen, Ox, are you going to tell me what you and your father were talking about, or am I going to have to . . .?" She left it hanging—or she couldn't think of anything strong enough.

"Mom, we were just talking. Nothing important, I can't even remember what it was."

"They were only talking," Sally said. I realized she was quite tight.

"What do you know about it?" Mom asked her.

"Enough to stay out of it," Sally said.

"But you aren't staying out of it," Mom told her. "You're horning in."

"Didn't mean to," Sally said. "Sorry about that."

"I'm worried that he's going to do something rash," Mom said to me.

"Like what?" I asked her.

"How do I know? I just have that feeling . . ."

"What *can* he do?" Sally asked her. "Cut off your allowance?"

"No!" Mom said. "He wouldn't dare."

"Then what are you worried about?" Sally asked her. She was tight, but she could think.

"He can be so unpleasant," Mom said. "And so petty, especially in money matters."

Sally cackled. "You mean he *does* cut off your allowance!"

They argued it back and forth, and finally Mom admitted that was right. She can never be honest straight off.

"Well, why don't you divorce him?" Sally asked, standing up. "I've gotta go," she said to me.

"I don't have grounds," Mom said sullenly.

"You must have, you've been married to him so long. Too long, I'd say. Problem is, he's probably got even more grounds. If you go after him . . . countersuit, lousy settlement. Right?"

"Even if that was true, which it isn't, you shouldn't say it in front of Ox."

"He doesn't care. Probably heard everything, anyhow. Right, Ox?"

"I suppose so," I said. Then I stood up, too. "Can I go now?" I asked Mom.

"Go ahead," she said wearily.

"I'll go with you," Sally said.

I walked out, trying to get away from her, but she was right behind me.

"Drive me home," she said. "I'm tiddly."

"How will I get back?"

"Use my car. Or take one of the others. Cars are no problem."

"I'm supposed to go to the B&T for lunch."

"I'll feed you."

I wouldn't have gone with her, but then Mom came along and wanted me to do something for her and it was the only way out.

2

I DROVE THE CAR—an old Buick with a busted muffler—and Sally combed her hair.

"Beautiful day," she said.

I didn't say anything.

"I said it's a beautiful day," she said.

"Yes, it is," I said.

"You're a funny one," she said. "Something very odd about you." She was quiet for a minute. "My first husband . . . no, Harry was my second . . . Harry was strange, too. Used to get up in the middle of the night and read books. Asked him about it and he said it was the only time he could concentrate."

"Maybe it was," I said.

"Maybe it was," she said. "Probably just wanted to get away from me. You don't like your mother, do you." It wasn't a question, she said it without raising her voice at the end.

"I like her all right," I said. "She's hard to get to know."

"That must be it," Sally said.

The Brackens lived in an old house off South Ocean Boulevard. There was a lot of shrubbery around it and vines all over it.

"Grim," Sally said, "but we call it home."

A tired-looking butler was wandering around inside, and Sally went past him without a word.

"There's sandwiches on the patio," he called after her.

"He doesn't need to tell me that," she said. "There are always sandwiches on the patio. We're famous for them. You go out there and I'll join you. But don't wait for me."

I went out on the patio and found the sandwiches. There was some other stuff, too. Cold vichyssoise, and a lobster salad. I was hungry, so I started in. The sandwiches were beef and ham. Everything was all right, except the lobster salad smelled bad, so I skipped it. Sometimes they keep those lobster salads for days—even weeks. The cooks are afraid to throw them out because there's usually an economy drive on.

Sally had changed when she came out, and she had a fresh drink.

"I wish he'd change his shirt," she said, and I guess she meant the butler.

"You don't remember Fifi Widener," she went on. "She was something."

She talked like that, going from one subject to another, and starting in on people you never heard of.

"It was fun in the old days," she said. "I was a kid then, in case you're wondering. Now I'm forty-one and not too unhappy about it. . . . My father shot himself after a bad night at Bradley's. Did you know that? Of course, that was just the last straw for him. He was a marvel at losing money. . . . He was second-generation Palm Beach. I'm third . . ."

She rambled on and on, and I kept putting away

those sandwiches. She didn't eat a thing. She talked and I ate, and it wasn't as boring as it sounds. The patio was shaded and a couple of old fountains were playing and it was very peaceful. She had a voice that didn't have any hurry in it, and was sort of a background noise itself. The whole atmosphere was a lot different from our house, where everything is new and everyone is always rushing.

My mind sort of drifted away and I wasn't listening to what she was saying until she raised her voice. "Ox, are you listening to me?"

"Sorry, it was so peaceful."

"I was asking you if you're happy."

"*Happy?*" No one had ever asked me that before in my life.

"Yes, happy."

"I never thought about it."

"Then perhaps you are." She got up and wandered around on the patio. "It's nice here," she said, "but one does get bored."

"That's what they say," I said.

"I'm not going to stay here this fall. I'm going to New York."

"Uh-huh."

"New York is dirty and noisy. Why would Sally Bracken leave beautiful Palm Beach and go to dirty New York?"

I didn't say anything, and she went on. "Let's say I have my reasons. My reason." She came and sat down again. "Actually, I'm going on an errand of mercy. One of my ex-husbands . . . you never knew any of them, did you?"

"No." Dad says no one ever knew any of them, they came and went so fast. Three months was about the average. She could really get them in and out.

"Doesn't matter. Probably better. This one, the one I'm talking about, was . . . is Davenport Blossom, not a bad fellow, really. His friends call him Bones, for some reason never clear to me—he's not thin—and he has nothing but friends. Gives you the picture. He's gifted, really he is. Writes books, does columns. And is so perturbed about our four-footed friends, especially the ones who live in Africa. Likes the ones with wings, too, but four feet come first. Founded the Friends of African Animals, and everyone who's anyone is a member. One thousand a year. Not cheap. Doesn't your father belong?"

"Probably." Dad belonged to every organization in the world that had anything to do with wildlife. It was his big interest. Now that he had all the trophies he wanted, he didn't want anyone else knocking those animals off.

"Anyhow, Bones Blossom—friend to all the world— is in something like trouble. The Friends of African Animals has collected about eight million over the past few years, and a quick audit of the books last week showed two or three million missing. Bones, not the best businessman in the world, is responsible to the board of directors before too long. If he can't come up with some explanation for the official auditors he's in very hot water. Follow me so far?"

"Sort of."

"When in trouble, who does he call? Lawyer? Accountant? One of the great tribe of friends? Negative. He

23

calls a retiring ex-wife who wouldn't know a balance sheet from a . . . cash flow projection. Why does he do that? Because he has to talk to someone about it, and he can't talk to anyone up there because they might blow the whistle on him. Lots of sniveling, but the message was clear: Help me. And I'm going to."

She stopped and waited, but I didn't say anything.

"I'm going to because he's a decent old fool, and because . . . well, if anything is worth an effort, I guess the animals are."

"I guess so," I said.

"When I came over today I was going to mention it to Barry, but your mother grabbed me and then he went off somewhere. I thought he might be interested in helping."

"He might," I said.

"I'll call him later," she said. She put her glass down and looked at me without saying anything for a moment. Then she said, "Unless you want to tell him about it."

"I don't understand it that well," I said.

"It's really quite simple," she said.

I was thinking that I wouldn't mind dropping it on him, because it would give him something to stew about outside the house instead of in, and that's a lot easier on everyone.

"Well, I could give him the general idea," I said, "and tell him to come to you for the details."

"That's it," she said. "That would be just fine." She got up and yawned. "Time for my siesta. Aren't you lucky you don't need one at your age?"

She was wrong, but I wasn't going to tell her that.

I was on my feet then, and she was looking up at me.

"You're huge," she said, yawning again. "How did you get so big?"

"Heredity. My grandfather was six-eight. Plus clean living, of course."

"Of course. But as we say, size isn't everything." She leaned against me. "I'm woozy . . . time to go bye-bye."

I had to hold her up a little to get her moving. When we got to the stairs, she thought I was someone else, because she said, "Not tonight, cowboy," as she started up.

When she'd gone a few steps, though, she turned around and said, "Sorry, Ox, it's just that I'm woozy. Be all right later. Don't forget to talk to Barry."

"I won't."

"Take any car you want."

And then she went the rest of the way up without looking back.

3

I PICKED OUT AN OLD Bentley in the garage and started to back it out, but a chauffeur with no shirt on tottered up and insisted on doing it. We had quite a tussle before he'd let me go off alone, but he finally gave in.

"Watch the tires," he hollered after me, as though I was going to Los Angeles or something.

I went to the B&T and had a club sandwich there and thought about Sally Bracken and how busted everyone was in Palm Beach. But still how much better they were, in some way, than people anywhere else. And more with it, for the good old 1970s.

Dad was out when I got home and I didn't see him until next morning, which was a Sunday. He had about an average hangover, the kind he's so used to that they don't bother him at all, and he just ate up the stuff about Bones Blossom and the money missing from the Friends of African Animals.

"Men like Bones Blossom deserve help," he said. "He's done great work."

"That's what she said."

"Maybe this is it," Dad said softly. "Maybe this is the chance I've been . . . an opportunity for growth . . ."

He hardly knew I was there.

Then he snapped to and jumped up. "I'm going right over and talk to Sally about it," he said in an important way, and went off in a big hurry.

"Take the Bentley back," I yelled after him. But he didn't, he was too excited.

He must have spent most of the day over there. When I saw him again, that Sunday evening, he had every-thing mapped out, and he nailed me to pour out the whole scheme. He and Sally had had a long talk, and then they had called Bones Blossom and had a long talk with him. The result was that Dad was now an executive in Friends of African Animals—or FRAAN, as they called it. I knew that meant he'd agreed to sink a lot of money into FRAAN. The only way Dad ever got into anything was to buy in. Being vice-president in charge of public relations—he had some title like that—meant he had to go to New York.

"I'm leaving next week," he said. "Going to rent some-thing and stay there until the job is done."

I couldn't believe my good luck. He was going to be gone for months.

"And you're coming, too," he said.

My heart didn't just sink. It went to the bottom and stayed there, and took all the rest of my organs with it. Every time I ever left Palm Beach everything either went wrong or got so boring you couldn't stand it. As long as I was in Palm Beach I could always get away from pressures, but when I got out there I was trapped. In Palm Beach I could get away from Dad when I had to, for instance. In New York I'd be with him all the time. It was too much. I was so stunned by the idea that

I couldn't even begin to argue. I just stared at him with my mouth open.

He thought the look on my face meant I was for it, because he clapped me on the shoulder and said, "I'm glad you realize what an opportunity it is for you, too. New York, Ox—plays, concerts, the cultural center of the country. Maybe of the world. You'll see and do things you'd never have a chance to do here. That's one of the reasons I decided to go—the great break it is for you."

"Dad, I . . ."

"Don't thank me now. Time for that later, when you have all those advantages under your belt. And if you're worried about school, don't be. They don't care here about your leaving, and you'll have your own tutor there."

"Dad, I . . ."

"A wonderful young man. Name's Parkinson. Relative of one of Sally's husbands. She arranged the whole thing. Remarkably efficient woman when she gets going. She agreed with me that you should come, by the way. Anyhow, Parkinson has superb credentials. Rhodes scholar, and studied at the Sorbonne, too. You'll get all the languages you need."

"Dad, will you . . ."

"I asked you not to thank me. It's something I should have done for you a long time ago."

I never even had a chance to argue. My whole life was ruined in five minutes and I couldn't do a thing about it. The only cold water I could throw was to ask him what Mom thought about it.

His face sort of fell then. "I haven't gone into it with

28

her." He thought it over, anticipating all the howls, and then his face hardened up again. "But there's nothing she can do about it."

He was right, but she gave it some try.

I was upstairs when they started, and you could have heard her on Worth Avenue. She gave it to him for being a fool and handing out money to Bones Blossom—she claimed it was a half million—and for thinking he could be an executive of anything, even FRAAN. And for spending more money going to New York. And for not allowing her enough money when he was throwing it with both hands. She gave it to him slow but boiling hot, and she's an expert.

He took it all—I guess he figured there was no way out—and then he said, "You don't understand. But that doesn't matter, because I'm going to do what has to be done whether you get it or not."

"What a joke," she said. "What a joke. And taking Ox, that's the final joke. What do you want him for? You've always liked to make these expeditions on your own."

"Ox needs to see the world," he said.

"Who's going to keep an eye on him?" she asked. "You?"

"His tutor, young Parkinson, will be in charge."

"I'll bet. And where did you find young Parkinson?"

"He's . . . he's a relative of Sally's."

"She seems to have provided a lot."

"Well, Bones is an ex-husband."

"She doesn't care anything about ex-husbands. Only about new ones. If she can find any she hasn't been married to."

"I think you're being unfair."

"You can't be unfair about Sally."

"If I knew you felt that way, I wouldn't have agreed to . . . work with her."

"What do you mean, 'work with her'?"

"Well, she's going up to New York herself . . . to help Bones and FRAAN . . . and she'll be helping . . . I even thought she might help take Ox around. She offered to, and I thought that was very kind of . . ."

"You mean Sally's going along on this junket?" Mom's voice was like a whip.

"She's not going along . . . with me, with us, if that's what you mean. She has her own place up there, she . . ."

And then Mom blew. Sky-high. They were at it for hours, and I stopped listening. I did hear some crashes later, but no screams.

By morning things were calm. Mom was even cheerful. That meant she'd gotten him to let her do something, or to give her an extra chunk of money.

"I don't envy you," she said to me.

"You have no idea," I said.

"I'll be thinking of you," she said.

"I wish I could keep from thinking of myself," I said.

"I'm sorry you're depressed."

"I'm not depressed. I'm numb."

She told me she'd be going to Buenos Aires while we were gone. I didn't ask why.

"And I'm going to have a good time while the two of you are having a very boring time."

"I hope you do."

She was my mother and I would have put my arms around her if it could have done any good. But I'd found out a long time ago that it couldn't. She lived in her own hard little private world and didn't want anyone else coming into it. Dad had a hard little private world, too, but he got tired of it every so often. That didn't make him better, but it did make him a little different.

The afternoon before we left I walked along the beach and said good-bye to the place in my own way. Palm Beach was the only steady friend I'd ever had. Always the same, you could depend on it. It was strange walking in the wet sand, thinking about how my hands were tied. It was a waiting game for me, I knew that. And outside of that, not much. I'd do what I could when I could, that was about it. That and what came from those times when you saw something different, really different. They didn't come often, but you had to be ready for them. You had to be ready and you had to pay for what you got out of them. That was it, that was about all there was.

4

DAD AND I FLEW TO New York from West Palm. He had about ten trunks to check and there was a lot of fuss about that. Sally was flying up with us, and she had a problem with her luggage, too. One of her bags was smelling up the whole airport, and the checkers had to open all of them until they finally found the trouble. She had left the top loose on a bottle of some French perfume, and it had all run out on her clothes.

"Won't be wearing those ensembles too often," she said. "All right for cocktails in a sewer, but that's about it." She didn't care about clothes and things the way most women do.

The ride up wasn't any trouble. She and Dad talked about animals and how mean people were to them, and I sat in another seat. There was a girl sitting next to me reading a book. She put it down pretty soon, though, and told me how people were starving all over the world, and wouldn't use birth control. She got excited when she talked and her tongue kept getting mixed up with her teeth. I knew she was going to bite it sooner or later, and she finally did.

Bones Blossom met us when we landed at Kennedy, and he was a little different than I had expected. Big and soft, with a lot of wrinkles. He shook hands with Dad and kissed Sally, and then we all piled into a rented limousine and headed for a place called Locust Valley on the North Shore of Long Island. Bones had rented a house for Dad there.

"I think you'll like it," he said. "It's right next to one of the Waterlukker places, Myrtle Grove. Nothing like the size of that, of course, but very attractive. Sunken living room. Eight bedrooms. Thirteen acres. Belongs to a man named Lochmann."

"You know, I have a place on Long Island," Dad said. "At Easthampton. But it's too far to commute."

I'd never heard about that place, but didn't butt in with any questions.

Then they talked about the problems at FRAAN. Dad was loving every minute of it. He was leaning back and nodding like some judge on the Supreme Court, and then pulling his lips together and looking out the window while he considered his decision.

"We'll find the money," Bones said. "I'm sure of it. Don't look at me that way, Sally, I didn't take it. Look at this suit." He held up a sleeve and it wasn't too clean, and had threads hanging at the cuff. "I live like a pauper. Well, why shouldn't I? I am a pauper, after all. Sally helped me find that niche in life," he said to Dad, and they all laughed. He was cheerful about his troubles.

That Long Island is something. Everything looks worn down—the cars, the people, the houses . . . even the sky. The part we were going to is supposed to be the best, with trees and breathing room—a lot of people from Palm Beach live there—but it's got something worn down about it, too. It's only about thirty miles from Manhattan and maybe that explains it.

The place we were using was on Goose Hollow Road, and the chauffeur had a hard time finding it, because all the roads twist around there until you can't tell where you are. Sally wanted to stop at Piping Rock for a drink, because we kept driving past the entrance, but Dad and Bones wouldn't let her.

We finally found the right end of Goose Hollow Road, and then the place itself. The sign on the road said Severn House, and under that it said Lochmann. The sign was small, and hard to read. We rolled in and up to the house. There was a man out in front stuffing a rug into the back seat of a car. When we piled out, he came over and said, "I'm Winston Lochmann," with a nervous smile. He was about forty-five and had a lot of dandruff on his collar and looked worried behind the smile. Dad and Bones told him who they were and who I was and a very little bit about who Sally was, and we all stood there in front of the house. It was early in November, and the sun was weak but still a little warm. The air itself was mild, and very different from Florida air. Dry, with smells in it.

"I wouldn't have rented the house to just anyone," Mr. Lochmann told Dad.

"That's right," Dad said. He hated that kind of talk.

Mr. Lochmann wanted to explain how everything in the house worked, but Dad told him he could do that later.

"I should tell you about the servants," Mr. Lochmann said with a little giggle. He acted as though everything was funny. "They . . ."

34

"We're rather tired," Sally told him, beating Dad to it. "Let's go over those details when we're fresh, shall we?"

He finally got the idea and left and we went inside and wandered through the place. It was big and gloomy.

"Lochmann is a bachelor," Bones told Dad. "Had a lot of money once, but lost it all in painting."

"Come again," Sally said.

"He thought representational painting was coming back," Bones said. "Bought all he could lay his hands on."

Representational painting is the opposite of abstract. It means you paint what you see, and it looks that way. It's the way painting used to be, before Picasso and the rest of them got going. You see it in museums a lot. And in a few private houses, like Mr. Lochmann's. He had it everywhere. Paintings of flowers and animals and people and landscapes, all over the place. And the attic and basement were full, too.

I'd never seen much of it before. In Palm Beach people go for what they call impressionist painting. That's about halfway between representational and abstract. Most of it comes from France. Dad says thay have factories there to turn it out, but he lets Mom buy it anyhow.

The big thing at Severn House was the sunken living room. The floor of it was about four feet below the level of the rest of the ground floor. It was a big room, with plenty of Oriental rugs and lamps where the light came out the top.

"Nineteen-twenties homey," Sally said.

I left them and went out into the kitchen. It was old-fashioned, with a tile floor and a restaurant kind of gas stove and a refrigerator with four doors and the motor on top. I opened one of the refrigerator doors and could see there wasn't much food inside. A couple of sticks of butter and a bowl with some tired salad in it, and a serving plate with four or five slices of ham. There wasn't much of anything else behind the other doors. The whole refrigerator was so big that the little amount of stuff on the shelves made it look emptier than if there'd been nothing at all.

While I was standing there wondering how we were going to survive, the door to the back stairs opened and a little short man came in. "I was Hans," he said to me with a heavy German accent. "I was the butler here. Who were you?"

"I was Ox Olmstead," I said. It was hard not to talk like him.

"Hox?"

"Ox."

"Why were you so big?"

"Because I wasn't so small."

He nodded his head, and then turned around and hollered, "Carmen!"

A woman's voice said, "Coming," from a long way off.

"Carmen," he explained to me. "She was my wife from Argentina. I make her housekeeper. She was good at it. You were knowing Argentina?"

"No."

"Nice place. I was there . . . um, ten years. It was being after the war. You were renting this house?"

"My father did. He's out in the front."

"I better say hello. I was hoping he was affording to eat. Mr. Lochmann couldn't."

36

He trotted out, and I opened the back door and looked at the garage and the trees. I was standing there when Sally came out into the kitchen.

"Cheer up," she said. "You're going to love it here."

"I know it," I said.

"We'll have this place humming."

"Have you met Hans?" I asked her.

"I have. He came down into the sunken living room and said he was there. He really does something for the sunken living room. Being no taller than it is sunken makes it seem even more sunken, sets it off."

Carmen showed up then, and she was not exactly what you expected. You thought she was going to be Spanish, being from South America, but she was as German as Hans. The only difference was that she was big. She had on a starched uniform, but there was a rip in the back of it.

"I will be surely baking bread," she said to us. "I will be surely taking yeast and baking bread. Just give me the little money and you will be smelling fresh bread."

She was wringing her hands and seemed very nervous. We found out later that she was scared to death of Hans.

"Let's leave the bread for a bit," Sally said. "Why don't you show me the whole house. Everything. Linen closets, furnace, wine cellar . . . bring your keys."

"We never had a bad word with Mr. Lochmann," Carmen said. "He was kind to us, and we did our best for him. Money was the only problem."

"It usually is," Sally said.

I slipped out the back door and left them there to straighten it out if they could.

Severn House had been a pretty pulled-together place once, but it had gone downhill. There were weeds on the tennis court and holes in the net, and cracks in the wall of the swimming pool, and the stables were empty and needed paint. I walked away from the house, through the woods. The leaves were still falling, but the trees were almost bare.

I was following a path that wound around through the woods and finally ended up at a chain link fence and a gate. The gate chain had a padlock on it, but it was hanging open. I slipped it out and went through. There were the same kinds of trees on the other side, but more evergreens, and the underbrush was all cleared away. It was like a park, just the trees and the meadows.

I pulled the gate to and put the lock back and started walking through the meadows near the groves of trees. There wasn't a sign of anyone around. You felt strange walking there, it was as though you were in another world. Part of that came from the pale sun and mild air and late fall warmth. And the smells in the air of dry leaves and evergreens, and others I didn't know. It was strange and different.

I kept going and finally got to a road. It wasn't narrow, the way you'd expect a road to be on an estate, but almost as wide as a regular two-lane road. The asphalt was thick and black. There was everything but a line painted down the middle.

I walked along it, and it was rising all the time. Finally it crested on the top of a low, rolling hill and the whole place was spread out in front of me. And at the same time, a voice said, "Hands up."

5

I TURNED AROUND and there was a girl walking toward me, coming from behind some shrubbery. She was wearing a kilt and a sweater with a high neck. She was tall, for a girl, and very thin. She was about my age.

"You haven't put your hands up," she said seriously.

"You don't have a gun."

"Guns are just for punctuation. What counts is the command."

She was up to me now and still looking very serious. Her hair was long and very dark and alive. Her face was tanned and dark. You couldn't really say if she was beautiful or not, but you felt she was. I mean, she had a face you couldn't take your eyes off.

"If I put my hands up I might not get them down," I said. "My shoulders might lock."

"You wouldn't want that to happen," she said.

"You're right."

"Then you don't have to put them up," she said. She bit her lip. "But you have to do something."

"Why?"

"Part of the form. You can't just walk in and do nothing."

39

"I'll walk out if you want."

"No." She laughed. "Where did you come from, any-how?"

"Next door. Severn House."

"You're visiting Winnie Lochmann? Really?" She acted as though she couldn't believe it.

"My father's rented the place for a few months."

"Rented Severn House?"

"That's right." She seemed kind of slow about taking it in.

"Why did he do that? No, don't tell me. Don't tell me anything. Let's leave it a mystery. It's much better that way," she said confidentially. "If you try to clear up a mystery, you always find it isn't worth it. Isn't that your experience?"

She was looking at me seriously, and I was thinking she was sort of nutty. I've seen so many nutty people that I can spot them even if they're only a little bit gone. The way you can tell is that you never feel natural with them. They can even be fun, but there's always a feeling of strain. I was feeling that strain while we were talking, and so I automatically said to myself that she was a little nutty.

Well, I still don't know if I was right or not. Some-times I think I was, and sometimes I think I wasn't, and sometimes I think I was and I wasn't—because she was and she wasn't. And most of the time I just give up and say I don't know. If she was a nut, she was the least nutty nut I've ever known; and if she wasn't a nut, she was the nuttiest non-nut I've ever known. It even came to me in a more far-out way than that once, when I was half asleep and I thought: If she is a nut, she isn't; and if she isn't a nut, she is.

There have been other people like that, I guess, especially in the old days. My friend Steve Lattimore told me a little while ago about the play called *Hamlet*, where Hamlet has everyone so confused that they don't know if he's the sanest or the maddest. Even he doesn't know. That's what really gets it going, when they don't know themselves whether they are or not.

But there's a lot of difference between reading about it in a book and actually running into it in life. You can walk away from a book—at least I can, and most people except real readers can, too—but you can't walk away from a live person who's like that. At least I can't. I couldn't then and I still can't. Couldn't walk away and couldn't figure it out, and still can't.

Everything she said stayed with you, that was another thing. She had just said, "If you try to clear up a mystery, you always find it isn't worth it. Isn't that your experience?" And it was then that I thought she was nutty. But her question came back to me, sort of laughing at me. I tried to clear up the mystery and I couldn't. So I might just as well not have tried. That wasn't my "experience" then, but it turned into my experience. I mean, if someone came along now and asked me the same question, I'd say yes so fast they'd think I'd been waiting to say it. And they'd be right.

And she was right. She knew it wasn't worth it to try to clear up a mystery, and she knew that was the experience you came away with if you tried. And if she was so right—then and later—about so many things, then how could she be nutty? I don't know, I honestly don't. Maybe the answer is that she wasn't. Not at all.

It's all very confusing. Right down to the word "nutty" itself. It's supposed to be an insulting word, and she's the last person I'd ever want to insult in any way. I could say that I shouldn't call her a nut, even in thinking about her—that if I had to think that way, I should use some other word, like "unbalanced." But those words wouldn't fit her, they're even more insulting. It was never a favor to her to pretend to be polite.

Even so, I still haven't said it right. That's the problem. You never could get anything right about her, in any way. I still can't.

Anyhow, to go back, she asked me the question about my experience, and I said, "I haven't had a lot of experience with mysteries."

"You haven't? You're lucky."

She started walking slowly down the road, and I walked with her. She hadn't asked me to, but I would have felt funny not doing it.

She stopped after about a hundred yards and turned and smiled at me. When she smiled she was another person. "You've never been here," she said. "Let me give you the verbal tour." We were still up above the place, looking down over all the buildings and lawns and gardens.

"Spread out below you is a small slice of the kingdom. Total acreage of this slice is two hundred and eight, still quite a chunk on Long Island. The main house has forty-seven rooms, and holds a priceless—shall we be coarse and say a ten-million-dollar?—collection of art. The pool house is that building to the far right. Minor but indicative detail: as you swim, you can feast your eyes on remarkable French tapestries, lifted in their entirety from some monastery in Picardy. The guest houses—one there, where I'm pointing, there are others out of sight—are . . . well, let's just call them minor masterpieces and let it go at that." She stopped and cocked her head at me. "But you don't want to hear all this."

"I don't mind. Who does it belong to?"

"Lizzie Revere. I'm sorry, I thought you knew."

"I still don't know. Is that your grandmother? Or mother?"

She laughed. "I should say not. I'm Cinderella here. You'd know Lizzie better by her maiden name. She's a Waterlukker."

I remembered then that Bones Blossom had said Severn House was next to one of the Waterlukker places.

"You do know who the Waterlukkers are?" She was looking at me with her forehead wrinkled up. "The sentimental favorite among America's richest and most powerful families?"

"I've heard of them."

"Good. Then we can forget about them." She sat down on the grass. "They're very unimportant people, really, even if they're supposed to be so important. Pompous, not too bright. Actually, Lizzie is the most interesting of the whole bunch, because she's so mean. Don't you like really, really mean people?"

"Maybe it's an acquired taste."

"Won't you sit down next to me?"

"Sure."

I did sit down and she was quiet for a moment. Then she said, "You may notice that I haven't asked you anything about yourself. It's not only that there's no point in meddling with mystery, but because I trust you. Don't ask me why, but I do. Without getting heavy about it."

I was looking down at all those perfect lawns and flower beds and thinking that she had problems.

She followed my eyes and said, "What if I were the Devil, and had brought you up here like he brought you-know-who to you-know-where, and I was offering you all of it for you-know-what?"

I didn't know exactly what to say, so I played along. "It wouldn't be enough."

"That's what they all say," she said. "At first."

"It wouldn't be enough," I said again.

"It's nice that you know that," she said seriously. She looked sad and chewed her lower lip. "I wish my father knew that." I was beginning to get the idea that she was something of an actress.

"My father is one of the Waterlukker serfs," she went on. I thought she meant one of the gardeners or something, but she didn't. She had the trick of almost reading your mind, because then she said, "I don't mean a literal serf. He's not down there cutting hay. He manages some of their money. He's an investment counselor. And they own him body and soul. . . . No, just body, he doesn't have a soul. Or if he ever did, he gave it up long before I was born. He must have thrown in my mother's at the same time. Package deal. Little bonus."

Down below, you could see people doing things, cutting grass, weeding, washing cars. It was like a picture by that painter named Breughel. He's the only old painter whose name and style I can always remember. We looked at a lot of paintings in an art class a year ago, and he was the only one I really liked. You can spend a long time taking in one of his scenes, because there are so many people and so much going on. He painted in

44

the sixteenth century, when people were outside and did a lot more together, like harvesting and celebrating.

"You're not listening to me," she said.

"I've heard every word."

"My first name is Arabella. Do you want to hear my last name?"

"I don't mind."

"I have two last names. One is official—Marlborough. The other is secret but real, at least it's real to me—Anorexia. On paper I'm Arabella Marlborough. But I'm really Arabella Anorexia. Isn't that a lovely name? It's like a poem by Edgar Allan Poe. Arabella Anorexia. Can't you see her? She's all in white and she wanders through a garden and she lives in an old tower, and there's some kind of strange love for her and by her, and she dies and there are a lot of lilies. Lilies and fog over water. 'My beautiful Arabella Anorexia . . .' "

She had been looking away from me and then she turned and looked full at me. Her eyes were wide and wet and fixed on me. It was the big moment. "It's not that pretty. I'm Arabella Anorexia because I had anorexia. Do you know what that is?"

"Yes." I did, too. It's where you don't eat and almost starve to death. Or you do starve to death, the way CeeCee Armistead did in Palm Beach.

"I went down to thirty-two pounds when I was eleven years old," she said. "I was in the hospital for almost a year. . . . My father came to visit me twice a week and told me how much it cost. . . . Do you know *why* one stops eating with anorexia?"

"No." That I didn't know.

"Because one is starved for affection. It's a way of

45

demonstrating that lack. A cry for help, a form of petulance, a kind of emotional sickness. They say it comes on the child because the parents are cold. But the blame doesn't matter. The important thing is that it means you're neurotic. It's a symptom of neurosis. Just like my opening my big watermelon of a mouth and telling you all about it is neurotic. Well, maybe not entirely. I didn't want to know you under false pretenses—can't sail under false colors, can we. . . .

"And even if I weren't neurotic, people would never let me forget. I'm the girl who had anorexia. 'Are you all right now? . . . My, you look so much better.' My mother, on the telephone to a friend, says, 'She's so much better, but of course there will always be . . . the aftereffects,' and then drops her voice when I enter the room, and starts talking about the weather."

"You can live it down."

"*I* can't. Maybe some people could, but *I* can't. I'm weak. Not physically—I'm completely recovered and they can't find a thing wrong. Weak in the other way, the worse way."

"Maybe you like to be weak."

"You're right, I do like to be weak. I know it's disgusting, but I can't help it."

I was thinking that she was giving herself airs and enjoying it, but I didn't feel the way you usually feel around people like that. It was as though she was all right at bottom, and all the weakness was only on top.

"Anyhow, let's not get heavy," she said. "There is the comic side to it, and I can usually turn the whole thing into a joke. If I'm Arabella Anorexia—and I am—then Dad is not Big Andy Marlborough, but Andy Candy—

the kid who will do anything for sweets—and Lizzie Revere is the Tin Lizzie, and Winston Lochmann is Winnie-the-Poop, and the whole valley turns into a magical dream, much more actual than what tries to pass as the real thing. We have the Tin Lizzie on the throne and Andy Candy holding down one of the towers, the one filled with very old licorice, and Winnie-the-Poop in cap and bells for entertainment. And the rest of the court— I know them all—and the serfs and peasants in the valley, and the ogres and dragons and monsters in the caves and up in the mountains, and the fights and the intrigues and the bad times and good times, thunderstorms and rainbows, and . . . finally . . . there comes into the valley the prancing steed and . . . let's skip a point-by-point description of the rider, we'll just say he has a deep voice and can knock off dragons the way . . . the way the Tin Lizzie can dispose of inadequate parlor maids . . . and he takes one look at Arabella and he says, 'Say, can you tell me the way to the palace?' And she's standing there in her dress that's made of laundered but unironed gunnysacks and wishing she'd hemmed it, to say nothing of ironing it, because she's not ready for this dazzling stranger in any way, and . . . well, you get it . . . "

I did and I didn't, but I wasn't going to say that.

She was full of life when she talked, Arabella was. Her hands drew forms—squares and circles and some you couldn't follow—and her voice was right there with what she was saying. I'd never heard a voice like it, low and vibrating. She'd snap one word off and then stay right on another one, dragging it out. All very clear, and without an accent. Or one so perfect you didn't notice it.

It was the most interesting voice I've ever heard. No matter what she said, you listened to it. It always made you think you were going someplace else to have a wonderful time. It seemed to promise you change and enjoyment. And then it delivered on the promise.

She talked in a modern way about what was going on, but you had the feeling often that she was from a long time ago. You see girls in old paintings and even in old photographs . . . I don't know, they're different, they're more in some way, they seem older and younger, they have something you can't put your finger on.

That was besides the little things, like the way she'd say, "Let's not be heavy," and "Let's skip a point-by-point description," when she was the only one talking. It's funny, but no matter how good anyone is at getting to you, you always notice the little things. Not in a mean way, but like seeing how it's done even when you're enjoying it. No, I'm wrong there. I never did see how the whole effect was done, because it wasn't staged—it was the way she was. All I saw, and it wasn't important, were a few little places where she wasn't consistent. But I don't know—even those may have been part of it.

I was thinking I'd had enough, that I wanted to be going, and she did that mind-reading thing she'd done before.

"Come again," she said. "Arabella will be glad to see you." I hadn't moved at all, but she knew.

"Are you always here?" I asked her.

"Always. Our house burned down a year ago, and the Tin Lizzie offered us one of the guest houses. We like it so much we'll never leave. We're in the Valley of the Nasty Green Witch forever, we are."

"Take it easy," I said. "It'll probably all work out."

She looked at me like she couldn't believe she was hearing such a dumb remark. Then her eyes widened. "Double-edged," she breathed. "Deep. Yes, it'll probably all work out. Of course, it has to, one way or the other. You aren't a fool, are you!" Her eyes were wet, but she was smiling. "You're not a fool. I can't believe it." She shook her head in a quick little way and turned. "Good-bye."

She started down the slope. She'd gone about fifty feet before she turned around and called back, "Can you find your way out?"

I waved my arm to mean that I could, and she turned back and kept going. From the back, with the "kingdom" beyond, she did look like some princess from a long time ago.

Then it came to me that the air suited her, too. I'd been wondering all afternoon what it was about that air, and then I knew. It was like Arabella, full of promises about enjoyment, what they call romantic. It sounds impossible that air could have that to it, but it did.

As I walked back, her effect started to wear off, and I told myself she was nuts. Don't kid yourself, she's completely nuts. But at the same time, I knew there was something else, too. There was something else and even if there hadn't been, there was the fact that she was fun, and you always have to respect that. I mean, when times are as tough as they are, anything or anyone who can make you forget it, even for a moment, is worth something. Worth a lot, to tell the truth.

6

WHEN I GOT BACK, my tutor was waiting to meet me. He was all alone in the sunken living room. He had medium-long hair and wasn't too sure of himself.

"You're Franklin . . . Ox," he said.

"Ox," I said. "No one calls me Franklin."

"I'm Ted Parkinson. Everyone calls me Ted."

"Is that what you want me to call you?"

"Why? Would you prefer something else?"

"I thought you might like 'Mr. Parkinson,' being a teacher."

"Heavens, no. Let's not be formal."

He had a little bit of an English accent, and just the trace of a stutter. He was shy, I could tell.

We started talking about what I was studying in school, and I could tell I was a disappointment there.

"I've never been a student," I said. "I just can't get interested."

"I'm sorry," he said. He seemed a little hurt.

"I don't mean to run knowledge down," I told him. "It's fine for people who like it. The way culture is. But it's not for me."

"But you have to be interested enough to achieve a

certain level," he said. "To get into college, I mean, and make your way generally."

"No, I don't." I said it as gently as I could, but it had to be straightened out. "I'm rich, Ted, and I'll never have to work, so I don't have to know anything." Except how to hold onto money, but I didn't mention that.

"That's a very shortsighted attitude," he said, getting red in the face and definitely stuttering. "What if your father loses his money?"

"Then I'll be a bum. Or give up in some other way."

"You're too young to know what you'd do."

"No, I'm not."

"But work is not a hardship, it can be fun."

"Maybe. But not when it's for money. All I mean is that I won't be a poor person, trying to stay afloat working at some lousy job, making money for other people. If I can't be free, I'll quit."

"But . . ." He was really upset, and I felt bad, because I didn't want to do that. I could tell he was nice and sort of all right. "What if everyone had that attitude?" he blurted out.

"What if they did?"

"Then the whole system would collapse."

"What if it did?"

"Then you wouldn't have any food or clothes or shelter—you couldn't live."

Now it was my turn to be confused. "I haven't thought it all out," I said, "but I know this system isn't that hot, anyhow. A lot of people say that. And if it did go down, I don't think it would mean there wouldn't be any food. But then people would be growing it for themselves, not to make money with."

He didn't say anything for a minute. Then he smiled and said, "Actually, you're not a capitalist. You're a radical."

"I don't know what I am." I didn't, either.

"You don't think work is bad if it's really work," he said, getting sort of excited. "You just don't like the idea of doing a job that has no meaning and only puts money in capitalist pockets."

That wasn't the real idea of what I meant, because I couldn't see work of any kind, but I wasn't going to contradict him. If it made him happy to put words in my mouth, then it was all right with me. I'd told him what I meant, as well as I could, considering the fact that I know what I feel even if I can't think, and from then on it was up to him.

"I think we're going to get along very well," he said, and he started drawing up a schedule for what we were going to study.

What was sort of funny about Ted was the way you could always see his mind work. As long as he thought I was just a rich kid, he was against what I was saying. But then when he thought I was a radical, the same words meant something else. He had to be for radicals because everyone around universities has to be if they want to relax and enjoy themselves. If they aren't, they end up fighting and arguing with the big majority of the other students and teachers, who are either radical or sympathetic. Ted told me that himself later, without really knowing he was doing it, when he described what happened to that Bill Buckley.

He was sitting there next to me drawing up that neat schedule, and everything about him—even his clothes—

was such a try, so hopeful. All you could end up with was that you didn't want to disappoint him, even if you knew you had to. Or that you'd make it up to him in some other way. I knew I was going to let him down as a student in a way he couldn't imagine. I had the idea, even that early, that I'd make it up to him in some other way. As it turned out, that wasn't really possible, but I would have if I could have.

We all had dinner together that night, and Dad was in pretty good form. He and Ted started talking about Oxford, and Dad said he'd been there. I couldn't believe he had, but it turned out he didn't mean he'd gone to classes there, only that he'd visited some English friend of his called Edderly who was a student.

"We'd met in Havana," Dad said. "Some pigeon shoot when we were both about twenty. Before Fiddle came in. We were visiting the Vonglers, I think it was. Asked me to look him up in England and I did. When I called his place, they said he was at Oxford and I went down there. I liked it."

"I did more than like it," Ted said. "I loved it. I wish I'd never had to leave. But, Edderly . . . that's the family name of the Marquesses of Hollen, isn't it?"

Dad said it was, and that his friend was the Marquess now, and had plenty of money troubles. "Says he's going to have to sell his place, can't keep up with the taxes."

"That would be Trune," Ted said. "One of the love-liest places in England," he explained to me, his English accent getting a little thicker.

"Poor old Bill," Dad said. "Hasn't got a dime."

Ted was looking at him in a funny way, but he didn't say anything.

53

"No one has," Sally said. "Not even you, Barry. You think you do, but you don't. It's all Monopoly money, and someday we'll have to wake up to that."

Dad only grinned. If Mom had said that to him, he would have blown up. But, of course, Mom didn't know how to say things. Sally did.

"They've already had to wake up to something in England," Dad said. "I like it, but it's finished."

Even Ted had to agree with that, much as he didn't want to. "But if I could afford to, I'd still live there," he said. "And if I were really . . . wealthy, I'd buy a place like Trune and live . . . well, that life." The wine had gotten to him a little and the English accent was rolling out.

"I do have the money," Dad growled in a pleasant way, "and I wouldn't spend ten bucks there anymore. Too depressing."

The dining room at Severn House was big and kind of empty. There were a lot of paintings by old American and English painters in it, mostly of animals. Ted told me the names of the painters once. A lot of the English painters had two names, with hyphens in between, the way the English do. There was one picture of a tiger in the jungle, stalking some sportsmen. They must have thought they were tracking him, because it was called *Hunting the Hunters.* The tiger was getting ready to spring, and the hunters didn't have a clue. You could spend a lot of time imagining what was going to happen next. When everyone else was talking, I used to look at that painting a lot. I got to know it about as well as you can get to know a painting.

Hans served dinner with a lot of noise. He didn't talk,

54

but you could tell he wanted to, and he puffed a lot. When he bent over behind you with a serving dish, he'd be going like a steam engine. When he was out of the room once, Dad said, "I have the feeling he's going to come in like an oil well," and we were all laughing and trying not to when he came back.

The food was better than I had expected. Now that Carmen had money, the refrigerator was full, and she was a good cook. Everyone else said her cooking was too heavy, but it was just my style. I'd never gotten *enough* heavy food before in my life, although I'd always kind of hoped to. The weather had something to do with it, too—you need a cooler climate than Palm Beach to bring your appetite to the peak. But now I was getting it, and it was a kind of dream come true. When everyone else was groaning about the dumplings and roasts and pies, I was putting them away. Of course, everyone made fun of me for eating so much.

"He was the biggest eater that ever I saw," Hans used to say.

"He was," Dad said once. "And that's what they've put on his tombstone."

"He was not gone yet," Hans said, kind of puzzled.

"Wasn't he?" Dad said deadpan, and Hans shook his head and gave up.

7

I THOUGHT IT WOULD take a long time for them to get organized, but it didn't. Mainly because Sally did the organizing. She decided we were all too helpless for her to move into Manhattan, so she just stayed. And when she got going she was a lot more efficient than you would have thought.

"I rather like being a housekeeper," she said. "Not bad having something to do in the mornings. Except drink, I mean."

Of course, she still forgot things every once in a while, the way she had with the perfume. She'd leave bathtubs running and the water would overflow bathrooms and soak through the ceilings below, and she'd miss appointments and let the cars run out of gas. But as Dad said, she was so easy to be around that you didn't pay too much attention to those things.

She'd get hold of Hans and Carmen early in the morning, and plan the day and the food with them. Then she'd wander around and see that the beds got made and that kind of stuff. She wouldn't take the first drink until noon, and then she'd only have one or two. In the afternoons she'd go over to Piping Rock and play paddle tennis or something. Then she'd come back to the house to change and get ready for the evening.

She was usually in a good mood, and she knew how to do little things for herself. She saw and heard things, too, and she knew how to tell you about them. "Saw another former husband today," she'd say. "Place seems to be full of them." And that was all she'd say. She knew when to stop, and never ran on.

Dad left pretty early every morning. I couldn't believe he was going to stick to a schedule, but he did. He didn't sleep in more than one work day a week, and for Dad that was unbelievable.

He started going into Manhattan on the train, like the regular businessmen out there. But he didn't like that, because of all the other people, and it was so slow, and the bullet holes in the sides of the cars. So he started driving in. But that got on his nerves, so he had a limousine pick him up and bring him home. Later there was something wrong with that, so he leased a helicopter. Finally there was the hydrofoil. That was the last.

I don't know what he did when he was in the city, but he claimed that he and Bones and the staff of FRAAN were straightening everything out. "We're getting there," he'd say. "Poor old Bones has really got everything in a tangle."

Bones came out to dinner every so often, and I sort of liked him. He had no side, and could turn a joke on himself. "I seem to have mislaid two million," he said. "Can't remember where. Thank God it wasn't animals, only dollars." He winked at me. "Animals are the best friends we have, never forget that, Ox."

"You sure you didn't lift the two million?" Dad asked him for the umpteenth time.

"I'm not brainy enough to be a crook," Bones said.

"He's got a point there," Sally said.

"Besides," Bones began, starting to show his cuffs again, "here is the proof of the . . ."

"Don't say pudding," Sally said. "The picture of those cuffs in a pudding is too much at dinner."

Winston Lochmann came to dinner once, too, and when Sally saw his dandruff going into the soup like salt she almost broke up. So did I. Mr. Lochmann noticed us and wanted to get in on the fun. He didn't realize it was his dandruff.

"You have secrets," he said, wagging his finger at Sally. "Well, so do I." Then he giggled, and we sobered up.

"I'm glad," Sally said. "We all need secrets." She told me later she thought he was sinister. "Watch out for gigglers," she said. "Always a corpse or two back there."

"But I tell my secrets," Mr. Lochmann went on then. "I can't keep them. I'll tell you one about Hans. His father was a dragoon in the German army, before World War I, and Hans calls him a dragon. Ask him about his father and listen to him say dragon. Side-splitting. I used to do it all the time. I'll ask him when he comes in again. You'll see."

"That would be cruel," Dad said. "I must ask you not to." Dad ordinarily liked cruelty—he did plenty of it himself—but he didn't like Mr. Lochmann. I got the impression that the feeling was mutual.

Later, of course, we all tried it out on Hans and it was just the way Mr. Lochmann had said it was. Hans would stick out his fat little chest and say, "My father was a dragon." Coming from Hans, it was funny, too. Mr. Lochmann was right, even though he was a giggler, and possibly sinister.

Dad and I got along pretty well, mainly because he seemed to like what he was doing and didn't have time to be sore at anyone. "Never knew administration could be such fun," he said. "Think what I've been missing all these years."

If he was having fun, I wasn't. At least as far as school was concerned. I started in with Ted every morning about nine. That is, it was supposed to be nine, but it usually turned out to be ten. Ted would be in my room about nine, trying to get me up, and I'd be stalling. Finally I'd roll out and go down to the kitchen, and Carmen would get to work and see how big a breakfast she could turn out. She used to look at me every morning like I was some pilgrim who'd just arrived in the holy land of his choice, or whatever they call it.

"Ox, I will surely be poaching eggs with Westphalian ham this morning," she'd say. Or, "Ox I will surely be heating the waffle iron this wonderful morning," and so on. The kitchen was always full of marvelous smells, especially the homemade bread that was always baking.

Hans would sit at the end of that big table in the kitchen with his chin propped on his hands, just watching me.

"It was a sight," he'd say to Ted, who'd be standing there impatiently, waiting to get going on the books. Of course, I'd be stalling as long as I could, taking my time over the ham and waffles and toast and biscuits and jams and eggs and sausage and bacon . . . it was amazing what she could do.

"It's not only the eating and the lateness I object to, "

Ted said once when we were alone. "It's Hans and Carmen."

"What's wrong with them?" I asked him.

"Surely it's apparent," he said, "even to . . ." He stopped and looked embarrassed.

"' . . . even to you,' you were going to say. I don't mind, Ted." I didn't, either.

"I didn't mean you're stupid. I meant you're too young to have had any experience or memory of what they stand for."

"Well, what do they stand for, except being servants? Hans is lousy, and Carmen is a very good cook, for me, anyhow. What else is there?"

"Ox, they're such obvious Nazis."

"Nazis? You mean they worked for Hitler?"

"They must have been involved in some way. Any German who fled to South America after the war had something to hide."

"But Hans is so dumb."

"He could have been a prison guard. Just the type. And some of those guards killed and tortured thousands of people."

"Then they must have a file on him," I said. "And if that was true, he couldn't be walking around the way he is."

"Oh, he could have changed his name. And the records get lost. And he was probably only a small fish."

"But why would Mr. Lochmann hire Germans who could be Nazis?"

"Probably doesn't realize they could be, and is just sorry for them as people. I understand he's a very kind man."

"But what makes you think Hans was a real Nazi? He never talks that way."

"Well, he wouldn't, would he? The giveaway is in being from Argentina. And the manner. The slimy, slippery German manner."

"You can be from Argentina without being a Nazi. There were lots of Germans there before World War II, Sally told me. Anyhow, Hans doesn't seem any worse to me than anyone else, just looking at him."

"You must be kidding," he said, staring at me.

"Everyone has something," I said. "Dad can be mean, Sally can drink too much, I can goof off. All Hans does is puff and goof off himself."

"But in such a repulsive way, in such a German way." He was starting to stutter. He stuttered when he got excited about something liberal, and slid into an English accent when he started into anything snobbish. You could tell which excitement was which without hearing the words. I've never known anyone else who did that; Ted was really unique.

"You sound as though you've got it in for the Germans," I said.

"I do. All civilized people find them offensive."

"You mean all Germans are offensive?"

"Very nearly all."

"And people like the English and French and Americans and Italians aren't?"

"Less so. Listen, Ox, the Germans tried to wreck civilization twice . . ." I let him go on and on, because it meant we wouldn't get to the books.

The funny thing was that we started off that way every morning. If it wasn't the Germans, it was civil rights, or inflation, or pollution. And he'd always end up telling me on what side of the question civilized people came down. I had to take his word for it, because I'd never known any civilized people. Except Steve Lattimore and his mother and sister, but they'd never talked about what was what. And Arabella—but she'd gone past civilization.

Anyhow, I'd tell Ted I believed him, and I did. What I didn't believe was that civilized people were always right. I didn't tell him that, though.

When we got through the business about civilization, we'd tackle math and English and stuff like that. But it was usually too late to do the job right. Ted would look at his watch after the civilization lecture, and see that it was already eleven or more. "Good Lord, it's ten past eleven," or whatever it was. "Where does the time go?"

I could have told him. On feeding me and talking me out of being a barbarian. He knew the first, but he didn't realize he was so much a booster of civilization that he'd always let the schoolwork go if he had a chance to sell it.

Anyhow, once we got down to the straight subjects there was never enough time to do them right. And besides, he was up against a kid who'd spent a lot of time with teachers and was a real expert. I don't mean to build myself up, but I never saw the teacher I couldn't slow down to a walk. Except maybe Mrs. Hollins, but she was so smart she wasn't like a teacher anyhow. Ted was a natural teacher, the kind of person who could never do anything else. And I was his first student, so he hadn't had time to work out a defense. Even when those real teachers do get some kind of defense, they're still so wrapped up in their own world that they don't know what's going on. That's why they're teachers.

Even Sally saw what his problem was. "Ted's like a vet who sets up shop and gets a gorilla for his first patient," she said to me one afternoon when we were alone. "He's standing there putting the Band-Aids away and the bell rings and he thinks it's a nice old lady with a sick canary. Instead in comes a circus trainer with six hundred pounds of trouble. 'He's got a broken arm,' the trainer says, 'and he's a little more upset than usual, but I'm sure you can handle him.' Cut to the vet's face."

"I'm not that bad," I said.

"You're not bad at all. That's the whole point. You're just impossible."

If I was, Ted never got it. He kept trying. And I kept trying, too, because I didn't want to hurt his feelings. But we never made it. We never even came close.

We'd knock off about twelve thirty. That was the end of the school day for me, except for the homework I was supposed to do. I'd try it, but it was usually too hard for me. And we both knew it was going to be.

In the afternoons I'd just loaf around, or take a drive, or go into Locust Valley with Hans, or someplace with Sally. Or go see Arabella.

Dad was always after me to go into New York, but I stayed away from it as much as possible. Arabella called the city "the feverish hive at the end of the expressway" and that was about the way I felt. The place really had nothing to offer, although I couldn't tell Dad that. If my grandmother had been there, I could have sat around her place. But she wasn't there in the fall.

I didn't know any kids on the North Shore, except

Arabella, and most of them were in boarding school anyhow. And after I'd had a look at a few of them, at Piping Rock and other places, I could see I wasn't missing much.

I spent quite a bit of time with Arabella, mostly on the grounds at Myrtle Grove, and I took her with me driving once in a while. She was home from school about three and I knew where to find her, a place near where we'd first met. She never suggested coming to Severn House, and I never asked her. What we had was private, although we never put it in those words, and we kept it that way without talking about it.

We talked about a lot of other things, though. She talked more than I did, but I did my share. And always enjoyed it, because there were enough surprises.

One afternoon she was complaining about the North Shore and I said it wasn't so bad, and she said, "Oh, you like this world—time rather stopped, Chekhovian lassitude . . . out on the island."

I didn't know what "Chekhovian lassitude" meant, but I got the idea.

"Well, it's actually terrible," she went on. "Frightening, once you know it. In the Locust Valley Pharmacy they call Valium . . . can you guess?"

I couldn't.

"Locust Valium," she said with a sad smile. "Gives you an idea of the consumption."

"I should get Ted on it."

"From what you tell me, he's already turned off." She thought about him seriously. "A tutor should properly be the impoverished remainder of the blind alley of an old family. Secret drinker, entirely indifferent to whether you study or not. Ted's not insincere enough or classy enough or far down enough to be a tutor. Also, even the perfect tutor shouldn't last. You should go through them like Kleenex."

"Dad wouldn't like that."

"Why not? It would mean you were serious about kicking people, a proper rich boy."

"He doesn't like anyone except himself to be serious about kicking people. And around animals, he won't allow any kicking, and that's what he's on now."

"The playboy with the sentimental moral sense," she said, smiling now. "Tom Buchanan with the occasional feeling of rectitude."

I asked her who Tom Buchanan was and she told me he was a playboy in a famous book and had looked and acted a lot like she imagined Dad did. From the way she described Buchanan, she was right on it.

Another time I showed her a card I'd gotten from Mom. It was one of those cards that are supposed to be funny, with a couple of mules on the front talking about sex. On the back, Mom had written, "On my way to South America. Weather lousy. Say hello to Sally." It was mailed from Jamaica.

Arabella lifted her eyebrows. "That's some mom."

"We think so."

"I don't know, Ox," she said, shaking her head and getting ready to tease me. "I don't know if a kid with a mom like that is going to make it." She was always telling me I'd never make it.

"I might fool you."

"With a mom like that? No, I'm wrong. Actually, that's a marvelous mom, you can't lose with a mom like that. What will *really* keep you from making it is that you don't have enough troubles."

"I don't like troubles."

"Sometimes they're unavoidable."

"People make a lot of their own troubles."

"And the sun goes down every night." She wasn't kidding anymore and she laughed a tight little laugh. "Tell me something new."

"It may not be a new way to say it," I said, trying to put it right, "but you'd be surprised how many people who know in their heads that people make their own troubles don't think it applies to them."

She thought that over for quite a while, and then she said, "You're obvious and you're not, at the same time."

And I felt a little sorry for her, for her carrying the load of knowing so much, and yet not knowing quite the right things for herself in the clutch. And for not taking care of herself.

But it wasn't often I felt sorry for her. And sorry or not, I always had a good time with her. I can remember those good times so clearly, too. What I said and what she said and where we were and how she looked, and the way she could go back and forth. She could be happy and carefree, with her hands making all those designs, and her voice purring along. And then sad, picking at a twig or a blade of grass in a jerky way. But even at those times I was enjoying myself. Not at her sadness, but because I knew it was only temporary.

And the weather kept holding, that was another

thing. Day after day with that sort of dry magic in the air. It wasn't until the middle of December that it got damp and cloudy and cold.

On one of those beautiful afternoons, I drove her to Bayview, a little town on the water near Oyster Bay, and we walked along the beach. It was almost deserted, except for a few people walking their dogs and collecting driftwood.

The Waterlukkers came up, and she said, "Everyone talks too much about them, including me."

"Except you're funny about them."

"I put them in the magic valley, if that's what you mean. By the way, did I tell you what happened to them when the revolution came?"

"No."

"I'm sure I did."

"No."

"You're just teasing me. Only want me to open up the old watermelon and make a fool of myself."

"Let's hear about the revolution."

" 'All right,' said the complete exhibitionist." She got ready. "Let's see. When the revolution came," she said, making a few hand designs for heads going off in a hurry, "the Tin Lizzie and the rest of the crew decided to change their name to Barnyard and go live with the sheepherders in the high pastures. 'We're the Barnyard boys,' they said when they arrived, 'and this is our sister, Betty Barnyard.' 'Something familiar about you Barnyards,' one of the sheepherders said. But he couldn't remember what it was. The sheepherders let the Barnyards have an old shack with a leaking roof to live in, and they became assistant sheepherders, and thought they were so clever. 'We were smart,' Betty (really Lizzie) said to her brothers. 'All the other nobles are dead, but we survived.' It took about twenty years before Clem Barnyard (William Waterlukker in a former life) turned to Lizzie and said, 'Say, what's so smart about living in a leaking shack and chasing sheep all day long like a sheep dog?' 'That's right,' said the others, and they felt very foolish."

She stopped and I said, "What did they do then?"

"Not much. What could they do? All the beautiful people, as they had been called in the former life, were up there by that time—Lennie B., Jackie O., Andy W., Norman M., everyone—gone quite native and living *al fresco*. That means outdoors, for those listeners who are culturally deprived. They ate nuts and berries and slept in trees and hollowed-out logs and thought it was wonderful they weren't dead. And the Barnyards were a little afraid of the beautiful people, so they kept quiet about their discovery that it was for the birds. Or the sheep, I should say. So now—or in the near future—if you go up there, you see furtive figures in the underbrush, the Barnyards chasing sheep, the sound of . . . sheep bells and rain, leaking roofs, small parties in hollowed-out logs—very small parties, I might add . . ."

"Sheep don't wear bells."

"Arabella, the ancient crone telling this Homeric tale from her perch at the fire, is aware of that. She laid it as a trap for you, to see if you're still awake."

"She did not. She forgot. She was running down."

"What if she did forget? Does it spoil the effect?"

"Not to me. You're better than Homer."

"You only say that because you don't know who he was."

"I'm not that ignorant. He's the one who wrote *Silas Marner*."

"Wrong again," Arabella said. "That was Dickens. Homer wrote *Bambi*."

"I've had enough of this smart talk," I said. "Let's get something to eat."

We went to one of those little seafood places across from the beach and I had a double order of fried clams. Arabella didn't have anything.

"The revolution has made him hungry," she said. "Wants to get filled up before the peasants take everything away."

"I'll give them these clams, too," I said.

She laughed and then she was silent for a long time. For so long that I looked over at her. She was looking back at me. We sat there looking at each other, and finally she said, "Are you trying to stare me down?"

"No."

"Then why are you looking at me so hard?"

"I don't know—because you're looking at me, I guess."

"I have to look at you . . . like I have to talk. Just another compulsion, I suppose."

I nodded my head. "Probably."

"You're impossible." Then she laughed. "But you're not stupid—you know what my trouble is."

"I do?"

"Of course you do. But you won't admit that. Good Lord, Arabella's getting heavy again!" She was upset under the joking.

She started to get up, and I said, "Wait a minute."

"For what? Are you going to eat another bushel of those things?"

"No. I just wanted to tell you that I do know what your trouble is."

She sat down. "Well."

"You like me and you're shy about saying so."

"That's right," she said slowly. "I've been burned about liking people."

"You're safe with me," I said. "I like you, too."

She thought that over carefully. "You do, don't you."

"Sure I do. Otherwise I wouldn't spend so much time with you."

"I've liked you from the beginning," she said.

"So have I."

"Well, why didn't you say so before?"

"Wasn't the time."

"You mean I had to say it first? What a male . . . whatever."

"Say pig."

"Not while you're eating."

"I'm finished. Let's go."

She was quiet in the car going back. When she got something new to work on, she was like a squirrel with a nut. She took it off into some secret place and turned it around and around. I liked that about her, too.

8

AT NIGHT WE ALL HAD DINNER together at Severn House. Dad and Sally and Ted and I, and whoever else happened to be there. Once a week or so they'd have people in for dinner, or go out themselves. But usually it was quiet and we all had a pretty good time. Dad was right in his element being a big shot all day, and that put him in a good mood every night.

On the weekends he'd play golf or go sailing or shooting, and sometimes Sally would go with him. Mostly, though, she stuck pretty close to Severn House. Only she called it "Severance House." Or "Splitsville." It was some kind of pun or joke.

"I'm really a homebody," she said to all of us one night at dinner. "A homebody with a fondness for strong drink, but still a homebody."

"You haven't been drinking much here," Dad said. "Almost thought you were taking the cure."

"Not quite that bad," she said. "But there has been a certain amount of drying out."

Ted was looking a little shocked, the way he always did. The husband of Sally's that he was related to wasn't a big holder, and Ted's own family was even further down, so he wasn't used to being around the rich. But I

71

knew that for all his talk, he found them a lot more interesting than he found people who were civilized.

He liked to gossip about them, that was one way I knew. He was always talking about this person or that in Locust Valley, and who they were related to and what they were doing. And the first thing he read every Sunday in the *Times* was the society section.

Of course, his big interest was Lizzie Revere and the other Waterlukkers. He was really excited about living next to a Waterlukker, and talked about them all the time, in a backward way.

"They say she has four hundred million," he said to me. "That's indecent. Don't you think so?"

"It's only money," I said.

"But with people starving in Asia and Africa—it's disgusting!"

"If she gave it all to them, it would probably only buy enough rice to keep all those Asians and Africans for two minutes."

We were killing time after my breakfast, and if he wanted to talk about Waterlukkers I was ready to stay with him all morning.

"That must be an extraordinary estate she has." He'd forgotten about the people starving, and his eyes were envious.

"Probably," I said. I never told him I went over there.

"She and the rest of them pretend to be public servants, but that's just a front," he said, working himself up. "They live like medieval princes. That's where their hearts are, in conspicuous consumption."

I asked him what that was, and he told me it was consuming just to put on a show.

72

"That's not all, either," he said. "They're not so pure as they seem. Jonathan . . . the one in . . . well, I should spare your tender ears."

"That's a dirty trick."

"All right, he's a homosexual. A very secretive closet queen, but the secret's gotten out. I hope I don't shock you."

I told him he didn't. Ordinarily, Ted liked homosexuals because he could talk about their rights. But he got so excited about the Waterlukkers that he forgot that.

Sally knew he was a snob, and liked to tease him and get his English accent going. It was right up there with getting Hans to say dragon.

"Lizzie Revere called," she'd say to Dad at dinner. "Some sort of Sunday afternoon tea and concert. Want to go?"

And Dad would look at her like she'd lost her mind and say, "I'd rather wrestle with a vulture." That was a favorite expression of his. Ted asked him about it once, and he said, "Have you ever smelled their breath?" Of course Ted hadn't, so it was a short conversation.

Anyhow, there Sally and Dad would be turning down an invitation to go over to Myrtle Grove, and Ted would have given an arm to go, and it was all in his face.

The Waterlukkers seemed to run through everything. Like the night before it all started, the night Dad said, "You won't believe who's living over at Myrtle Grove—Big Andy Marlborough." He stopped and looked around, but the name didn't register.

"Come again," Sally said.

"You know Big Andy," he said to her.

"Negative," Sally said. "More input."

"Big Andy and I hunted together in Africa . . . um, when I was still hunting. Liked him, but felt sorry for him. Always under his mother's thumb. Never enough money, same old story. Anyhow, he's an investment counselor, and I gave him some work. No good, lost money for me, so I had to stop using him, and haven't seen him in years. Today I ran into him at the Racquet Club and he tells me he's working for Lizzie Revere and living next door in a house on her property. Something about his own house burning down. He's had a hard time. One thing after another. Has a daughter who's had anorexia. We had a couple of drinks, and I felt so sorry for him I asked if he'd manage some stuff for me again. It'll make a few thousand a year for him, and he jumped at it. This kid evidently cost him a fortune—he's still paying for it. What the hell is anorexia, anyhow? I mean, I know what it is, but how does it get so expensive?"

Sally told him.

9

OF COURSE, the next time I saw Arabella she was all ready for me.

"Isn't it nice," she said. "My daddy knows your daddy."

"For a long time, I guess."

"I didn't realize how rich you are," she said. "And how grateful Andy Candy would be for the bone—or should I say bonbon?—thrown to him so magnanimously."

She wasn't joking, she was upset about her father. It made me uncomfortable, and she knew it.

"Listen," she said, "I wouldn't be this way about my father if I didn't have reason. Don't you understand? I wanted to have a father I could love. It's worse than that—I can't really live if I can't love a father, my father. That's why I'm sick all the time . . . was sick. Don't you see, if there was anything there to love, I'd take it and love it and shut up. But there's *nothing*. He's weak and vicious and silly, and on and on, but even that wouldn't matter if he had one square inch for me in his heart. But he doesn't . . . "

Her eyes were filled with tears and she looked miserable. I didn't know if she was the best actress in the world or whether she felt it all. Or something in between.

"Now I've spoiled your afternoon," she said. "I didn't mean to do that."

"Forget it"

"All right," she said. And she did. Which is unusual because most people can't do it that fast.

"I want to show you something," she said. "I've wanted to for some time. But the moment was never right. Today it's perfect. Come on."

We were walking in the woods at the edge of one of the lawns near the main house, and she turned and took me by the hand and led me across the lawn toward a side entrance. We went in, across some halls full of art and up a back stairs.

"Quiet," she whispered. "We're in the servants' wing."

I would have known it even if she hadn't said it. There's a special shade of green that rich people have their servants' wings painted. Halls, rooms, everything. It's a color that the rich themselves wouldn't be comfortable with, so they think it's fine for the people who work for them.

Servants' rooms are always sad, too. In big houses they sit in those rooms waiting to do the next chore, smoking and watching television. The sadness is not only in the rooms, but even in the way their things are laid out. A new coat on the back of a chair in the middle of all the bad furniture and green paint doesn't make the whole picture brighter, but more hopeless.

I always try not to look when I'm passing rooms like that, but you can't help it.

Arabella noticed that I looked, and said, "Terrible, isn't it. But don't forget they put up with it." She was right, and that's something I've always known, too.

We passed through a connecting door and came out on a landing above the entrance to the dining room. Arabella crouched down behind the banisters and I did my best to do the same thing. When you got down you could see directly into the dining room.

There was an enormous long table in the middle of that room, and lots of pictures on the walls and a fire going in the fireplace. The maids and butler were setting the table for a dinner of about thirty people, and overseeing the whole operation was Mrs. Revere.

She was a thin woman, medium height, and looked about seventy. The only two things you really noticed about her were her voice and her walk. She walked with a stiff back and hunched forward, as though her back had been broken once. When she was outside with a cane and walking a little bit faster than she did in the house, she really did remind you of a witch. Inside a house she did, too, but not so much.

Her voice was basically what you hear around New York, sort of a drawl with the r's dropped. Then she had added a special whine of her own. The finished product went right through you.

"No," she was saying to the butler, "that is not where I want them." She was talking about some little silver bowls with mints in them. She shook her head in a way that said, "How can I have told you this so often and you still don't get it? I try and I try, but it never seems to do any good. How can you be so cruel to me as not to do what I want when I'm so patient with you, and always take into account the fact that you're a servant and not very bright?" It had all that in it and more. Besides the head shaking, she had a funny, tight little smile.

The butler was so nervous by then that he couldn't do anything right. His hands were shaking and he knocked over a water glass. It was empty, but he acted like he'd just poured a barrel of water over the whole table.

"Everything will be just right, Mrs. Revere," he kept saying. "Everything will be just right."

"How can everything be just right, Austin, if everything is so *very* wrong now? I don't know why I'm so foolish as to even *try* to give a dinner party with the . . . I'm not blaming you or the rest of the staff, Austin. I know you try. But trying isn't good enough if you can't follow simple, clear directives. Now these glasses are all wrong. They should be here."

She changed the position on a glass, and shot a quick look at one of the maids.

"But I put them there because you told me to," the maid said.

"I couldn't have," Mrs. Revere said.

"But you did," the woman said.

"I couldn't have done such a thing," Mrs. Revere said with a kind of gentle deadliness. "I could never have done such a thing because I happen to know how place settings should be put down. I have even taken courses in the management of food from purchasing to . . . the actual . . . the table. How could I have gone against my own training and instincts and . . . the answer is that I couldn't have. You are mistaken, and I expect you to be sufficiently professional to admit it."

There was a long silence. All the other servants were

looking at the one on the spot, who was trying to keep control of herself. But her legs were trembling. You could tell it by the movement in her skirt. She opened her mouth to say something, to defend herself, because she had to believe that Mrs. Revere was telling her black was white. But then she closed it, because there was no way out. She either had to eat it or quit, and she didn't want to quit.

The other servants were looking at her without any sympathy. It had happened to all of them, and servants get so they don't care if it happens to someone else. Just as long as it isn't happening to them. Arabella claimed they actually enjoy seeing another one get it, because it means they aren't.

The silence dragged out, and it was terrible. Mrs. Revere was looking at that maid like she'd caught her stealing the silver. There wasn't a trace of mercy in her face or the way she was standing there. You got the idea that she could stand there until next year if she had to.

Finally, of course, the maid buckled, like she had to all along. She wet her lips and murmured, "I must have made a mistake."

"I can't hear you," Mrs. Revere said.

"I must have made a mistake," the maid said a little louder.

"Mistakes happen," Mrs. Revere said in that severe way mixed with a little fake kindness that all really nasty people have got down perfectly. When they get the victim helpless they like to play a little. "Mistakes happen," Mrs. Revere said again, "and I think you'll all agree that no one here is more aware of that than I am. Well, I have to be," she added with a little smile, "because there are so many of them. And I think you know that I never feel a mistake means the person making it is *completely* and permanently incompetent. Oh, no. But dishonesty and impertinence . . . those are different matters altogether. Those I cannot accept, and I think all of you know it."

She waited until they all nodded a little.

"Now, then, if that settles that, perhaps we can get on with the work we have to do here, and see if we can't be a little more efficient, helpful . . . and polite . . . and honest."

It went on and on, around and around that table. She found a way to get every one of them—there were five—going in one way or another. And they all had to own up to some "mistake."

By the time Arabella and I crept away, they were all reduced to nervous wrecks. And Mrs. Revere was still at it and ready for more.

"Nice?" Arabella asked me when we were outside again.

"Not nice," I said. "Makes you sick."

"You realize, of course, that the point of that scene is not the dinner party, but torturing the 'staff.' Also, that Austin and the rest are perfectly capable of doing the dinner. They've been doing dinners for years. Everything she pretends to find fault with ends up exactly as it was. So she's *only* there to cause trouble."

"She's something, all right."

"And that's only a part of her day. In the morning she tortures her secretary and the people involved with the charities and good causes she gives money to. As well as her bankers and accountants and relatives. In the afternoon she plays with all the people who work here—the ones you saw plus the rest of the inside servants and cooks, and the gardeners and chauffeurs. And Big Andy Candy. In the evening there's poor old Revere himself and whoever is around for dinner. It's a full day."

"How do you get along with her?"

"No better than anyone else, but I stay out of her way. How do you think you'd get along with her?"

"No chance."

"The Wicked Witch of the North Shore is something special—so antisocial she makes a rattlesnake look like a snuggle bunny. But seriously—isn't it incredible how they put up with it?"

"People are scared, Arabella."

"Yes, but I thought Americans didn't crawl like that. The crawlers are supposed to be over in Europe."

"I don't know. I guess Americans can crawl with the best of them."

"John Wayne, where are you?" she said.

I knew that what really got to her was her father down there on his hands and knees, too.

"Ox," she said seriously, "let's do something."

"Like what?"

"I don't know. Save the day . . . man the boats . . . cause some trouble, somehow, get back at the Tin Lizzies."

"There's enough trouble around without causing any. Besides, let's not get heavy."

"That's mean."

"Wasn't intended that way."

"Making fun of me, mimicking my poor little conversational crutches . . . I wish I could be out of school the way you are."

"I'm not out of school, I'm with my tutor all the time."

"Baloney."

"I study hard."

"Baloney. Extra-thick baloney."

"As hard as I can."

"You're a loafer and I want to loaf with you."

"Come on over. Ted would like to talk to someone with some brains."

"Oh, Ox, you just said I had brains!"

"You do."

"If I have brains, how come I'm living at Myrtle Grove? How come I have Andy Candy for a father?"

"That's just the luck of the draw. That doesn't have anything to do with brains."

"I can't have brains," she said as though it had just occurred to her. "I'm going crazy."

"That's right," I said. I never argued with her when she got like that.

"I'm a freak!" she howled, dancing around. "Ox, an ordinary freak or a Jesus freak? Tell me which to be!"

"Stick with the ordinary freaks," I told her. "If you're a Jesus freak, you have to pray."

"I like to pray," she yelled, still dancing. "I pray to unknown gods. And a few known ones, too. I go to all the churches."

That interested me, because I'd never known a kid before who went to church. She calmed down and told me about going to a Russian church in Sea Cliff, about ten miles from Locust Valley, and a Greek church in Manhattan, and lots of Catholic and Episcopalian churches. "I go in and get on my knees and pray," she said.

"What about?"

"What do you mean, what about?"

"For special favors or what?"

"For guidance, you clown. For an explanation of the riddle of the universe." She was dancing around again. "For the answer to you, Ox Olmstead, as well as to the whole cast, including, of course, the Tin Lizzie, good old Lizzie Revere herself, the Wicked Witch, the Supreme Torturer, et cetera. I could have prayed all night," she sang, following the tune of that song about the girl who could have danced all night.

It was then that I looked up and saw Lizzie Revere standing there, leaning on her cane and ready to go off.

10

ARABELLA DIDN'T SEE HER for almost a full minute, and kept on going with stuff about how she'd be a servant and live in a green room and get kicked by Lizzie every day, and pray all night that she'd get kicked harder. I couldn't think of anything to do—I was sitting on the ground with my back to a tree and I couldn't get Arabella's eye. So I just waved my hand at Lizzie. It was about all I could come up with, to act like it was a show or something that Arabella was giving and that I was asking her to have a seat and enjoy it. Of course, she wouldn't do that, but the idea was to make a joke out of it.

Finally Arabella did see her, and that was pathetic. She stopped singing and jumping around, stopped like she was shot, and her face crumpled. You hear about faces crumpling, but you don't see it much. Arabella's really did do it. It just dissolved into nothing, and turned white at the same time.

Mrs. Revere was so tough that she didn't speak first. She was going to make Arabella speak, to explain the disgraceful way she had been hopping around and calling her awful names. Arabella was ready to do it, I could tell, and I could have let her, but somehow I didn't want that to happen.

So I started to my feet, and on the way up I said, "We don't want any," to Mrs. Revere. I said it like I was sore.

She swiveled those eyes around on me, and then back to Arabella, still not saying a word. You had to admire the way she did it. She was tough, and not afraid of a thing.

"We don't want any," I said again. "We don't care what you're selling."

"Who might you be?" she asked me. I was thinking that with her head forward and swiveling around, and her hunched back, she looked just like an old turtle. An old turtle, but full of fight.

"I'm Ox Olmstead," I said. "I don't buy. I sell, but I don't buy."

"You must be unbalanced," she said. "And just what are you . . ."

I didn't let her finish. "You mean you're not selling apples? Gee, I was looking forward to turning down an apple seller."

It was finally getting to her. "You're impertinent," she said. "And you're a trespasser. I'm going to have you arrested."

"I'll leave," I said.

"You'll go to jail," she said grimly, snapping her jaw shut. She took a little whistle out of her pocket and blew it.

"I think I'll be running along," I said to Arabella. "Want to come?"

"I don't know," she said. She was scared to death.

"Come on," I said. "Don't be frightened of that jail talk."

Two gardeners burst through the shrubbery and Mrs. Revere said to them, "Hold that young man until the police come. I'm going to get someone to telephone them."

"He may be young, but he's awful big," one of the men said.

"Do as I say," she said.

"I'm going peacefully," I said to them. "She just wants to get the police to be mean. I haven't done anything. If you try to stop me, I'm going to fight back." I started for the road to the gate. "Come on, Arabella."

"Stop him," Mrs. Revere said in a clear, sharp voice. She never did get to a yell.

Well, they had no choice, so they came at me. I'm only seventeen and never in condition, but anyone who's over six-six and weighs quite a bit more than two-fifty and is strong in the arms is hard to handle. I got the first one by the shirt below the collar and held him up and out where his arms couldn't reach me and his feet were off the ground, and kept walking. The second one was dancing around just out of reach, trying to get in a shot at me.

"I can carry both of you," I told the second one, "so don't come too close if you don't want a free ride, too."

It seemed more a joke than anything else, and I was almost starting to laugh and so were they. But then something happened to change it. I heard Arabella scream, and in the same instant I felt a white-hot flash go off in the back of my head. If I passed out, though, it was only for a second or so. Then I was down on all fours and rolling over while the man who had hit me with the shovel took another cut and the shovel blade dug into the ground.

I was a little dizzy, but I was sore. I reached out and got the man's ankle and pulled him up as I was getting up. Then I got his other ankle and whirled him around by the ankles until he was straight out at the ends of my arms, and going around in a huge circle. He let go the shovel then and it sailed past Lizzie like a missile. She never batted an eye. I got up all the speed I could and let him go.

He sailed up and away, squawking like a turkey, and ended up in the branches of a tree about twenty feet off the ground.

"He could have killed me," I told the other two, who weren't moving. I could feel the blood running down the back of my neck, and I was afraid to think of how bad I was cut. "He's lucky I didn't do the same to him. Now you two get out of the way or I'll show you what happens when I really get sore."

They didn't move or say anything, and neither did Lizzie. I guess the blood and what had almost happened to me had even cooled her off. It wouldn't have looked too good to knock off a seventeen-year-old—no matter how big. Even the Waterlukkers would have had trouble with that.

So I walked away, and Arabella came with me, saying over her shoulder, "I wonder who's suing her now."

As soon as we were away she said, "The back of your head is really a mess. Can you make it home?"

"Sure." I didn't know if I could or not, but thought I had to say so.

"I'll come with you to make sure you get there."

"I was going to ask you to come, anyhow. You can stay until Dad explains to your dad what happened."

"God, there's going to be a mess over this," she said, chewing away at her lower lip.

"There was nothing else to do."

"That's all right for you to say. You don't live here. What she'll do to Andy Candy! And what he'll do to me!"

"Maybe we can head him off."

"I doubt it," she said. She was rigid with fear.

It was sort of too bad that she was a coward, I was thinking. And that she didn't seem to understand how I'd tried to get Lizzie's attention off her and onto me, and that that was why I'd gotten slugged. She was so wrapped up in her own problems, I thought, that she didn't see most of what was going on.

But whenever you thought a thing like that about her, you found out later you were wrong.

We went through the gate and along to Severn House.

"I've never been here before," she said. "I should, though, seeing that I shall be the happy chatelaine of all these seedy acres someday."

I didn't know what chatelaine meant and didn't care, but I asked her because I thought if we kept talking it would help keep me from passing out.

"Sort of a Lady-of-the-Lake type, runs the castle. What it means in my case is that I've been promised to Winston Lochmann, Winnie-the-Poop. I've been sold by

Andy Candy for an unspecified number of five-pound boxes. The wedding is scheduled for my eighteenth birthday. Big times in the valley on that festive day. Unlimited beer for the peasants, all in their native dress, champagne in the big house, bonfires, dignified hilarity . . ."

"I can't follow you. You mean you're supposed to marry Mr. Lochmann?"

"That's the general idea."

"But they can't make you do that."

"They can't? Don't be naive."

"They can't."

"They can. For one thing, they have my vote. Half-hearted, but still a vote. After all, it would get me away from Andy Candy, the Tin Lizzie, and the rest of the bunch."

"Not much improvement."

"Oh, I don't know. He's not so bad. And probably easy to handle, being so old."

She was looking at me with hard eyes that didn't make it.

"He's not too well off, though, is he?" I asked her. "Unless representational painting comes back."

"His brother's got quite a bit—enough—and is such a climber that he'll finance Winnie-the-Poop for marriage into the Social Register." She looked at me as though daring me to say something about that.

"If it's what you want," I said, as though I didn't care. In a way, I didn't. Anyhow, you can never tell people anything when they're telling you something.

"It would cause a lot of trouble, anyhow," she said in a softer way.

My head was starting to hurt and I didn't say anything.

She seemed upset that I didn't argue with her. We
walked the rest of the way without saying anything.

11

HANS ALMOST FAINTED when he saw me. He let off a string of German, and then he collapsed into a chair. Carmen was no good, either, and Arabella didn't know where anything was. I couldn't get at the cut myself, and I don't know what would have happened if Sally hadn't been there. She drifted into the kitchen and took charge right away.

"Let's wash it," she said to no one in particular, and got them all going on water and towels and soap and the rest. She did the washing and it hurt, but her hands felt like she knew what she was doing. She didn't ask how it had happened. She only said, "Looks like the guillotine is coming back." That's that thing they had in France to cut people's heads off.

When she got it clean, Hans came over for a look and collapsed again.

"It's not that bad," Sally said. "About six stitches, I'd say. Have to get a surgeon on it. I'll drive you to the hospital."

Arabella wanted to come with us and Sally said that was all right.

In the car no one said much. Sally wasn't going to ask

anything, and Arabella wasn't going to offer anything. Women pair off like that a lot of times. It doesn't mean it's permanent, though.

The hospital was in Glen Cove, about ten minutes away. A doctor and a nurse took me into an emergency room and sewed me up and took X rays. It didn't hurt because they gave me a shot of Novocain. The doctor asked me how it happened, and I said someone had been swinging a shovel and hit me. I didn't tell him any more than that. I could have said I slipped and hit my head on something, but I didn't know if we might have to use the truth someday. They make records of accidents and if anyone went back and looked, I didn't want to come out a liar, especially if we were trying to prove anything on Lizzie Revere. I didn't tell the doctor the whole truth, because if I had it might have dragged me into some action against Lizzie right then and there. I told him just enough so that I wasn't lying if the whole truth had to come out later.

"It's a very nasty cut," he said, "especially because of the location on the back of your scalp. Could have killed you. The X rays don't show fracture but you may have a slight concussion. You should stay here a couple of days under observation."

"I can't do that," I said. "But I can stay in bed at home."

He said that was all right, and they finally let me go. When we walked out, he thought Sally was my mother and started telling her about what I needed. Sally didn't argue with him and tell him who she really was, the way most women would have. She didn't argue with anyone if she could help it.

It was colder when we left the hospital, and almost dark. Sally and Arabella had found they had something to talk about while they were alone, and going back to the house they were at it hot and heavy. But it all sounded kind of artificial, about people and places.

I went upstairs to my room when we got back and Arabella followed me up.

I lay on the bed and she said, "I can't stand that woman."

"Who? Sally?"

"Sally. She's everything I dislike. And she dislikes me just as much as I do her."

"Sally's all right. She's a good friend. And easy to get along with."

"I suppose I'm not." She looked sad. "You're probably right—she's calm and easy and everything I'm not."

"You've got your good points," I said. I was almost asleep. It sounded like something you'd say about a horse, but I was too tired to care. She didn't answer and I drifted off.

When I woke up she was gone, but there was a note propped up near the lamp. I didn't feel much like reading anything, but I thought I should. Her handwriting was like printing, so it made it easier.

"The valley rings," it began, and I felt tired all over again, but I kept going. "Rings with tales of his exploits, the fierce stranger. The oldest inhabitants can't believe the stories. 'Gardeners in trees, indeed,' they whuffle. 'Impossible, fairy tales for infants.' But they are wrong, as always, because gardeners did fly, verily, verily. Through the air they sailed in graceful parabolas, and roosted in trees. Miracles came to pass . . . don't think I don't know, my extra-large friend, what happened and why. No one has ever done anything for me, and I was so overcome that I couldn't take it in. I still wouldn't want to try to say it to you, because I'm poor with words when I need them, like so many people who can spout them when it doesn't matter. So don't expect me to say it, but believe that what I write is what I know, even though I won't refer to it when we see each other. (Maybe someday, and I have a few other things to tell you, too.) I was wrong about Sally, of course, and I've gone to make my peace with her. See you when you wake. A. A."

At first I thought that the "A. A." meant she had some kind of drinking problem, but then I realized it stood for Arabella Anorexia. As for the rest of the note—well, as I said, it made me a little ashamed that I'd thought she hadn't known what was going on. The rest of it I didn't think about. Girls and women have their own ways of straightening things out for themselves and I never try to stop them.

I went downstairs, with that big bandage around my head like I'd just been in an automobile accident. It was after seven by then and Dad was home, sitting in the sunken living room and smoking a pipe. He was alone and reading a newspaper like a real businessman.

"All right," he said, folding the newspaper, "let's have it."

"That Mrs. Revere sicked her gardeners on me," I said. "Even after I said I'd leave. One of them tried to kill me."

"What were you doing over there?"

"Taking a walk."

"Trespassing."

"All right, but not enough for this sock in the head."

"What's this about throwing a gardener into a tree?"

"It was that or do something to him like he did to me."

"Did you actually throw him into a tree?"

"Uh-huh."

Dad got up and walked around. When he stopped he looked up for guidance, in his new style, and said, "How do I get a son who throws gardeners into trees? I could understand almost anything else, but is a man supposed to be ready for *that,* too? Isn't it asking too much?" Then he got back to me. "What about the girl? You've been sneaking over there to see her."

"Have you had a look at her?"

"No."

"When you do, you'll know she's not the kind of girl anyone sneaks over to see."

"Then why do you see her?"

"She's got troubles and I feel sorry for her."

"That's what always gets you into messes, isn't it. You're always feeling sorry for someone and the next thing you're in trouble. Not them—*you.* Why can't you leave people with troubles alone?"

"I guess it's my hobby."

"Get another one."

"I can't leave this in the middle. She's the daughter of your friend Andy Marlborough, the one who works for Mrs. Revere, the one you just gave some business to."

"I know," Dad said. "I've got that already. It doesn't mean . . ."

"She was making fun of Mrs. Revere when the old lady came up behind her. Now the old lady will take it out on the father and he'll take it out on Arabella."

"So what?"

"She's already had a bad time. It'll break her."

"How do you know that?"

"I just know."

"I still say, who cares?"

"I do."

"You can't afford to."

"Yes, I can. Even if I couldn't, I'd have to. I won't drop it in the middle."

"I wish you felt that way about people in your own family."

"Everyone in my family can take care of themselves."

He didn't say anything for a minute. "Or about your schoolwork, or some purpose in your life."

"I wish that, too."

"Then why don't you do something about it?"

"I don't know."

"What an answer."

"That's not the problem at this moment. I don't want that girl to be hurt. I want you to help me see that she isn't hurt."

"Are you crazy?" His face got really hard. "You want *me* to help you take care of some nutty girl? You're not playing with a full deck, pal."

"I'm not going to let him tear her apart," I said.

"He's on his way over here right now," Dad said. "He's going to pick her up, and there isn't a thing you can do about it."

"I'll do something."

"Ox, you've lost your mind."

I was wondering if he wasn't right. I was off balance in a way I couldn't ever remember being. I couldn't understand myself why I was out there so far in front of my own shadow, but I was in it too deep by then to back out. The funny thing was that Dad knew I wasn't going to back out. I could tell by the look on his face. He knew it and he wasn't absolutely sure that he'd be able to stop me.

We were standing there facing off when Hans came in. "Mr. Marlborough . . . " Then he saw me and my bandage. "Ox, you was OK?"

"Sure."

He made the sign of the cross on himself. That's what the old-time Catholics from Europe do in emergencies. They do it for good news as well as bad, and in situations where they don't know which way it's going to go. Not every single one does it, but the ones that do, do it all the time.

"I was feeling better," he said. "You were too young to die. That goddamned Jack Taffle at the Reveres' was hitting him *mit einer Schaufel!*" he said to Dad. He was really excited. "With a *shovel*, Mr. Olmstead. Jack was a German, too—well, his mother's father was—and he was hitting a boy with a shovel! That goddamned Revere woman! I was to be telling him! I guess you were calling the cops yourself, *nein?* I guess you were to have been revenging yourself. I guess Jack Taffle won't be to have been asleep tonight, *nicht war?*"

Dad, who hadn't been thinking of any of those things, and hadn't paid any attention to what had happened to me, was taken by surprise. He started to mumble something, and then he remembered that the great law of his life was that a good offense is the best defense, and he steamed right back at Hans.

"That's none of your business!" he bellowed. "You

stick to your job and I'll stick to mine! And how dare you use profanity when you're talking to me?"

Now it was Hans's turn to be surprised and he pulled himself right up to attention. "I didn't mean . . ." he began.

"That'll do!" Dad yelled. It was pretty funny watching him having to work so hard. "Forget it! . . . But remember what I've told you. Now what were you going to say about Mr. Marlborough?"

"He was here," Hans said.

"You mean he's gone?"

"No, he was waiting. I was from to be announcing him."

"Why didn't you say so?"

"I was trying to have been to with doing that." When Hans got upset, he could really tangle up the language, even more than usual.

"Then do it."

He made the announcement. "Mr. Marlborough was here."

"Then show him in."

"Yessir."

When he went out, I could see a couple of patches of dried blue paint on his black trousers.

Dad dropped into a chair and let his arms sag. "Now I know why people give up business. It isn't the day at the office, it's what you find when you get home."

"That's what they say," I said.

He looked at me, and I knew he was wondering whether he should say something about the crack I'd gotten on my head. He started to, and then he stopped, and I had to admire him for that. In my family no one ever shows any feeling for anyone else. It's probably good in a way because it's sink or swim for everyone. People from those families that are always falling all over each other are so used to it that they can't do without it when they get away from it.

In a family like mine, you get so you depend on getting nothing, and Dad would have really thrown me a curve if he'd showed sympathy. I could handle anything else from him, but I don't think I could have handled that.

12

BIG ANDY MARLBOROUGH came into the sunken living room like he'd been shot out of a cannon, big all right and with his hair pretty well gone. He was tanned, through, and so full of energy that he seemed healthy. He was in his early forties, like Dad.

"Barry!" he boomed at Dad. "How long has it been?" He grabbed Dad's hand and pumped it, and Dad looked kind of uneasy. They were both in suits and ties and you couldn't believe it was happening to Dad.

"Only a couple of days—not very long," Dad said. He might have wanted to say more, but he didn't have a chance, because Big Andy started right in.

"That's long in my book," he said, and then dropped that. "I'm here to straighten all this out. Big Andy is here and you can relax."

He was Big Andy to everyone, including himself, and he really believed he was in charge. All the time, even when he was eating it from Lizzie Revere or someone like that. He was actually sort of a failure in life, but he couldn't admit that in any way. "He came out of Harvard Business School absolutely sure he was going to succeed, and he can't believe it didn't happen," Arabella said about him, and I guess that covered it. His business life was a flop, but he had a few things to keep him going—the Marlboroughs were an old family in New York, and so he was socially pretty much on top and no one could take that away from him. And someday, when his mother died, he'd have a few million. So he just ignored all the rest and acted as though he had made a big success and was running everything.

"I'm glad I don't have to worry," Dad said sort of sarcastically.

"That's what we all want," Big Andy said. Sarcasm was a waste of time with him, he didn't get it at all. But something about the word "worry" being batted back and forth sort of got to him, because he frowned and looked vague for a moment. But it was only a split second, and then he was back at it, coming toward me.

"You must be Ox," he said, grabbing my hand and pumping it. He was a squeezer and he had a strong grip. I just let my hand go limp.

"My God, you *are* big. I thought they were exaggerating. Now, Ox, I know you're all right, because I know your old man is all right, but anyone can make a mistake. Slinging Jack Taffle into a tree was . . . did you really do it, you don't seem to have much strength in your hand. Guess you save it for those big moments, eh? Anyhow, Jack is really pretty sore at you, which I think you'll agree he has a right to be. Not as sore as he might be, under the circumstances. And Mrs. Revere is furious, and I don't think there's any doubt she has more than a right to be. So you're in real trouble."

He was still gripping my hand, and he had that big tanned face right under mine, and his eyes were trying to bore in hard. He was big, and I could tell he was a little upset that he had to look up at me. His teeth were huge and white, and he smelled of gin and cocktail onions. He didn't look a bit like Arabella.

"That gardener tried to kill me," I said. "He's lucky he isn't in jail."

Big Andy didn't even blink. He just laughed and turned around to Dad. "Did you hear that, Barry? Your kid doesn't understand the trouble he's in."

"Neither do I, to tell you the truth," Dad said. "*Your* daughter invited him over there. He offered to leave quietly when Lizzie Revere wanted him off, but she turned the gardeners loose on him. The one that hit him with a shovel could have killed him. Throwing someone like that into a tree is only funny. He didn't hurt him."

"Barry, Barry, Ox was on private property, Mrs. Revere's private property. He had no right to be there. Arabella didn't have the right to invite him, if that's what she did, because it's not her property. Mrs. Revere had the right to have him ejected. Especially when he was rude to her and didn't tell her who he was or where he was from. He resisted the gardeners and they had to defend themselves. Then he assaulted one of them. Open-and-shut."

"You're not serious, Andy."

"Big Andy couldn't be more serious. This boy's in very real trouble. Of course, Mrs. Revere isn't vindictive, and if Ox makes the right moves, she probably won't prosecute. But don't think she couldn't."

"What would the right moves be?" Dad asked softly. He's used to always having his own way, and he doesn't go for the idea that anyone else is more important than he is.

"I think a formal apology to her, and one to Jack Taffle—that's the gardener—plus a few hundred to Taffle. I can't promise anything, but I think that might do it."

Then Dad laughed.

"What's so funny?" Big Andy asked him.

Dad stopped laughing. "Why, I think you're full of shit," he said in a pleasant way.

Big Andy was still holding my hand and I could feel his fingers tighten. This time I tightened back.

"Barry, you're not in Palm Beach. This is New York. Mrs. Revere . . ." He looked down at our hands, feeling the pressure, and tightened some more. I kept right with him. "Mrs. Revere is a very kind woman, but there are limits to her kindness."

"Lizzie Revere is as mean as they come," Dad said, "and you know it as well as I do."

Big Andy tightened a little more when he heard her called Lizzie. I gave him that and added some. I have a lot of strength in my hands, and the sweat was beginning to bead on his head where it was bald.

"Let's not get nasty, Barry," he said. He wanted to say more, but now he was so far into the contest with me that he couldn't concentrate. He was giving it all he had and it wasn't enough.

"Say, what are you two lovebirds up to?" Dad asked, stepping over. Big Andy's breath was coming fast, and his head was really beaded. His hand felt like putty now, and I rolled the bones a little.

"Let him go, Ox," Dad said.

I did, and Big Andy shook his hand like I'd broken it. "Just tried to shake hands with him and he damned near tore my hand off. If that's a sample of his behavior, I can see why those gardeners have a beef."

"He tried to play strong man with me," I said to Dad. "I finally squeezed back."

Dad waved his hands impatiently. "Andy, you shouldn't get into anything physical with Ox. Act your age."

"I didn't do anything," Big Andy said. "He . . ."

So they went at it some more, and ended up in about the same place. Dad figured out that Big Andy's weak spot was Mrs. Revere. If she wasn't treated like royalty, it upset him. So Dad, who's as mean as they come when he wants to be, called her Lizzie and was generally nasty about her, which blew Big Andy higher and higher. And Big Andy figured out that what irritated Dad was to be told how much more important the Reveres were than the Olmsteads, so he worked on that. It made Dad sore, although it wasn't exactly a weak spot, because Dad is insolent enough at bottom to think he's as good as anyone, and probably a lot better.

Another thing that annoyed Dad was that his promising some work to Big Andy wasn't enough of a bribe—Big Andy was acting like he'd forgotten all about it, and when Dad does throw a bone he likes it to be appreciated. So he was sore for more reasons than one, and barked back. He wasn't defending me, but protecting himself. If Big Andy had played it better, he could have gotten Dad on his side against me. But he made too many mistakes.

It ended in a kind of a confusion, the way those

things always do. Big Andy was saying the Reveres were going to prosecute me, and Dad was saying he'd prosecute them.

"I'm disappointed in you, Barry," Big Andy said sadly, getting ready to go.

"Why?" Dad asked him in a kind of fake interested way. "Because I can't see an assault with a deadly weapon on an innocent kid as anything but just that? Because I think Lizzie Revere is boring and over-inflated, and I'm sorry she has you under her thumb?"

"You're all mixed up, Barry," Big Andy said, still sadly. He'd figured out by then that the sad, solemn approach was about his only way. It wasn't a bad idea, if you wanted to blow Dad up, because nothing made him sorer than to be patronized.

"You used to be all right," Dad said. "What happened to you, Andy? These Reveres have turned you into another person. I wasn't kidding—you *are* full of shit."

"There's no need to be vulgar," Big Andy said.

"Vulgar! From the Andy Marlborough who used to go into all the joints in East Africa and yell . . ."

"That'll do, Barry," Big Andy said, looking nervously at me. "Where's Arabella?" he asked, to change the subject. "It's time to go."

"She says she doesn't want to go with you," Dad said. "She wants to stay here and study with Ox."

I didn't realize until then that he must have talked to her while I was asleep.

"She's not well," Big Andy said, shaking his head. "She's very confused."

"Confused or not, she wants to stay here." Dad had the knife in and was enjoying it. And, like fighting with

105

Big Andy about the Reveres, he wasn't doing it for me but for himself.

"She can't . . . did she say *why?*"

That was what Dad had been waiting for. "She says she can't stand seeing you sucking around Lizzie Revere."

"She . . . she didn't say that, you're putting words in her mouth. Will you call her, or shall I get her myself?"

That was what *she* was waiting for, because she was right there at the top of the steps leading down to the sunken living room.

"If you want me, Big Andy, all you have to do is whistle," she said. "You know how to whistle, don't you ? You just put your lips together and . . . blow."

I didn't get it at first. But then the way she was standing there against a pillar in a kind of slinky way, and the fake sexiness she was putting into her voice, brought something back to me.

"I told you she was sick," Big Andy said to Dad with a shrug. He didn't get her at all.

"What *is* that supposed to mean?" Dad asked her. He was sort of sore, and I was with him, for once.

Arabella just stared at the two of them with big eyes. She wasn't going to explain herself, so I did.

"She's imitating Lauren Bacall in *Key Largo,*" I said to Dad. "It's an old movie on TV all the time. You probably saw it when it came out."

"I know the movie," he said irritably, "but what's the point?"

What had made him sore wasn't that she'd done an imitation, but that it wasn't the time or the place, and she hadn't done it well. And finally, it wasn't what a girl does to her father, especially with other people around. Her fight with Big Andy was serious enough so that she should have kept it serious. Doing a lazy imitation made the fight look silly and herself look stupid. It was all off, all out of balance and focus and the rest. When a nothing person makes a mistake like that, you don't care, because the person probably can't do any better—if they weren't awkward that way, they would be in some other way. But with someone like Arabella, who was such a something person, you did care.

I cared, and Dad cared in his way, because he had a feeling for gracefulness. Big Andy was too far gone to care about anything. He actually liked it when she did things like that, because it meant he was right, that she was crazy. But Dad and I were uncomfortable, and sore. I was sore because she'd let herself down, and Dad was sore because he didn't like graceful people who did awkward things and spoiled his sense of balance. I was sore for her and he was sore at her, if that makes any difference. He had only seen Arabella for a few minutes, when I was sleeping, but he knew she was naturally graceful, no matter how mixed up she was. He didn't know he knew it—Dad's all instinct—but he did.

Anyhow, there was Arabella being a lousy Lauren Bacall, and Dad and I being uncomfortable, and Big Andy loving it.

Suddenly she got it, she knew she'd made a mistake. And like always, she came through.

"No point," she said to Dad in her normal voice. "I was only playing the fool to relieve the tension. Sorry it didn't work—I guess I'm not as amusing as I thought I was."

"That happens to everybody," Dad said. His voice was rough, but she was all right for him now that she'd faced the problem and handled it.

"Well, Mr. Olmstead," she said to Dad, looking at him straight, "do I get to stay or do I have to go back?"

Big Andy didn't say a word. I guess he figured Dad would have egg on his face no matter what he decided, and he liked that.

"I can't turn this place into a home for runaway girls," Dad said with a laugh. "I sympathize with your reluctance to share Big Andy's company, but if I took you in here it would be kidnapping. How old are you?"

"Seventeen."

"How old does she have to be before she can run away from you legally?" Dad asked Big Andy, as though he was asking how General Motors was doing.

"I don't know," Big Andy said. It wasn't turning out quite like he'd expected.

"Eighteen," Arabella said. "But that's almost a year away. Anyhow, to be honest, I don't have the guts to run away and work and be independent. I'm weak, someone has to take care of me."

"Don't look at me," Dad said. He hates weak people, and the idea of being responsible for anyone is . . . well, it's everything he's against. So when she put them together, he was through. It didn't occur to him then that a really weak and dependent person wouldn't have said what she did, but he got the idea later.

That would have been it if Big Andy hadn't put his big foot in his big mouth again.

"No one could possibly take you on," he said to Arabella. "You're too sick. And you always betray the fact that you are. Come on." He grabbed at her elbow, and she pulled away from him.

I was right behind Dad, and he knew I wasn't going to watch her pulled out screaming. But as much as that, he couldn't stand Big Andy's complete lack of grace. Dad's a strange person in a lot of ways. Mean and selfish. But he moves well, and his voice is attractive, and he can be amusing. He's graceful, and he can't stand people who aren't. That's the real basis of all the trouble between him and Mom.

"You don't need to get rough," he said then to Big Andy. "I don't want a scene here."

"You stay out of this," Big Andy said, lunging at her again. She backed behind one of the pillars—they ran all around the sunken living room—and started to stick out her tongue at him, I could tell, but at the last moment she had the sense not to, and just looked frightened and cornered.

"Wait a minute, pal," Dad said, moving toward Big Andy. "This is my house, and I don't want this sort of thing going on in it. You go out and wait in your car and I'll be out with her in a few minutes. Now, move."

Dad can be tough when he wants to be, and he can be mean in a fight, too. Big Andy hesitated, but then I guess his idea that the Waterlukkers could do anything and if you worked for them you had the same privileges was stronger than anything else.

"She's my daughter and I'll take her out of here any way I want," he snarled. Even at that, he might have gotten by with it, but then he added the clincher. "No Palm Beach punk is going to tell me how to behave." You could count on Big Andy to do your work for you.

His back was slightly to Dad, so he never saw the punch coming. Dad was lucky and got him right on that spot on the jaw where they're supposed to go out, and he proved it by going out. Down and out.

He hadn't hit the floor before Dad was on the telephone to the police. "I've just been assaulted in my home. Yes, still here, we have him under control. Yes, I wish to prefer charges."

Dad knows every move in that situation because he's been through it so many times, on both ends. "When they're down, kick 'em," he says, and from his angle he's probably right.

"Will he go to jail?" Arabella asked with what they call relish.

"I'm not doing this for you," Dad said. "It's for my own sake. I could have Hans drive him home, but then in the morning he'd say I had assaulted him. I have to take the initiative."

"You really caught him," I said. I'd bent over to take a close look, and Big Andy was sleeping like a baby. His mouth was open and the gin and cocktail onion smell was very strong.

"What if he wakes up before the police come?" Arabella asked.

"Ox can sit on him. Now listen, young lady, you're the next problem. The cops won't book your father, he's too well known. They'll take him home and let him come down to the station in the morning and see if I want to prefer charges."

"Will you?"

"I'll see. Probably, unless he backs down. The point is that he'll be going home tonight sore as hell, and I'm going to tell the cops it's too dangerous for you, so you can stay here if they think it's all right."

Arabella didn't say anything, she just stared at him.

"Don't get any funny ideas," Dad warned her. "I'm doing this as part of my case against him, not for you. And it's only for one night."

"It's certainly better than nothing," she said in her lowest voice, her eyes down now.

"Maybe tomorrow things will open up," Dad said to her, with what was a gentle manner for him. "Maybe it won't be so bad for you at home from now on if Big Andy gets his feathers clipped."

She kept on trying to be sad, but she couldn't. She looked up, broke into that wonderful smile she had, and walked over to Dad.

"Say, you're all right, mister," she said, just like Lauren Bacall again, and threw her arms around Dad and kissed him.

I thought he'd blow, but he couldn't. This time was the right time to be Lauren, and she did it perfectly.

13

THE COPS WERE THERE in a few minutes, and
it all went just about the way Dad had thought it would.

"I can't believe Mr. Marlborough would have assaulted you," the sergeant said to Dad with a twinkle in
his eye. "He's such a nice man. A little noisy, maybe, but
nothing violent."

"Still waters run deep," Arabella said, but no one in
that room got those literary references.

"I'm not so sure," Dad said. "Sometimes these nonviolent types are the worst when they let go. Anyhow, all
I know is that he came at me and I had to defend myself."

"You sure did that," the sergeant said.

They got Big Andy out then. He could stand on his
feet, but he was still woozy. He wasn't saying anything,
and seemed to want to get home as fast as they wanted
to take him. While two of them loaded him into a squad
car, Dad arranged for Arabella to stay.

"I don't see how her own father can be dangerous for
her," the sergeant said, smiling at Dad like he knew who
was kidding who.

"Oh, if you feel that way, take her along by all means,"

Dad said indifferently. "I was only thinking of her safety. If Big Andy decides to go after her tonight with a club, it won't be on my head, Sergeant. It's your decision."

"Now, wait a minute," the sergeant said. "All I said was that I don't see how her father can be dangerous for her. I didn't mean it would be impossible."

So she stayed.

Dinner that night was really sort of fun. To begin with, Arabella was excited and full of life and spirits. Dad was surprised at himself and not unhappy about what he'd done. Sally was in a good mood, too, and Hans and Carmen were all for what had happened.

"He was deserving it coming," Hans said when he served the soup. "And going, too."

"I'm surrounded by Tarzans," Sally said.

"The valley has moved to Africa," Arabella said. "Big trees and trailing vines to swing from. The tomtoms beat all night, relaying their exploits to the farthest corners of the bush."

No one knew what she was talking about half the time, but we got the general idea and the details didn't matter.

She was taking it all in like a kid at a carnival, with her eyes going from one person to another and all over the room. I could see her looking at those paintings like she couldn't believe them. Her eyes were shining and she didn't miss a thing. "As you may have guessed, I don't get out very often," she had said to me once, and I could tell it that night.

Ted was the only one not in the general mood. I guess because the Waterlukkers were involved. And someone had been slugged, and he was nonviolent. Probably the worst thing was that we were like a bunch of political revolutionaries who'd just knocked over a bank and he couldn't stand the atmosphere. He always thought he was radical, but when it came right down to it, he wasn't.

Arabella fascinated him. He stared at her with his mouth practically open. The Marlboroughs were nowhere as far as money went, but they had an old name, and Ted thought that was even better in some ways than a medium-old name with lots of money, like the Waterlukkers, who'd made it all after the Civil War. The Marlboroughs were holding as far back as the Revolution. "Had a lot more then than now," Arabella had told me. "How's that for management?"

Besides that, her conversational style had him going. He was the only one whose vocabulary was anywhere near hers, so he understood more of what she said than we did. In one way, that is. In another way, he didn't get as much as anyone else, because he couldn't follow her imagination. Like the magic valley, or what she'd done with Lauren Bacall . . . he was too rigid to let go and just listen and get the sense behind the words.

She noticed him staring at her, and it made her nervous. She shot a quick look at me as if to say, "Is this tutor for real?" I could only shrug to tell her he probably wasn't.

From then on, she tried to handle him herself, and she did a lousy job. Arabella had trouble slowing down enough to handle dumb people like Ted. She thought you did it by speeding up.

Like then, when he asked her where the valley was before it moved to Africa, and she said, "Oh, it was right here. It still is—the trip to Africa was only temporary. It runs north and south, and a bit east and west, but not up and down. Gnomes, elves, trolls—lots of bridges for those trolls to hide under, can't have trolls without bridges—and the usual assortment of straights and magicals. Witches abound, and various other forms of wickedness. I'm a student witch myself . . . oh, yes, I'm in the valley, too, in very unfashionable clothes. Fetching and carrying for a big-time witch. Hall of Famer. There's very little goodness in the valley, just enough to keep it interesting. Like yeast in bread, though, it is the key ingredient . . . what would the witches do without it? . . . "

She went on and on, her voice so attractive and her hands flying around and her face sort of beautiful in the candlelight. But her eyes scared and all wrong. It was still fun, but now there was hysteria in it. She didn't know what to do with a dummy like Ted. Those staring eyes and that mouth practically open had her going. She was like a rabbit in front of a snake. I felt very sorry for her, because ninety-nine percent of the people in this world are like Ted, and she was going to have a rough time if she couldn't come up with a style for handling them. And herself.

I wanted to do something to help her, to get her off the hook. But I was sort of paralyzed myself, and couldn't come up with anything. It was Sally who finally put the brakes on. By that time, Arabella was talking so fast you could hardly understand the words themselves, let alone the sense of them. It was pathetic.

"Didn't you tell me you rode?" she asked Ted, cutting across Arabella.

"Well, a little," he said, not taking his eyes off Arabella. He wanted her to keep going.

"Arabella is quite a rider," Sally said. "Show jumping."

"Oh?" Ted said, more interested. "Out here?"

"All over," Sally said, not giving Arabella a chance to answer. "She's got a roomful of trophies. Where was it you rode, Ted?"

"Oh, I'm not in that class," Ted said. "But I did do some riding to hounds when I was at Oxford. With the Quorn. A friend of mine rode with them and he took me along a few times."

"Awful what they do to the fox," Dad said. He got what Sally was doing and was helping out, plus plugging his new love for live animals.

Arabella was about to open her mouth, but I was able to get my finger across my lips without Ted seeing and she shut up.

So he went ahead and argued about whether fox hunting was cruel or not, and from there Sally pulled him by the nose from one thing he'd done to another. As much as he loved drinking in what he called an aristocrat, he loved boosting himself in front of that same aristocrat even more.

It didn't take Arabella long to get the idea, and she started dropping in little questions herself, and listening politely to the long-winded answers. Now it was his turn to wonder why he was hearing so much of his own voice. But he couldn't stop—they never can.

I noticed, too, that for the first time since I'd known him he had both the stutter and the English accent going. I guess maybe it was because it was a snobbish and a liberal situation at the same time. Snobbish because of Arabella and liberal because he could give his opinions on everything.

It sounds mean, but it wasn't. The funny thing was that Ted was nice in a way. He wasn't vicious at all, underneath, and he didn't want to hurt anyone. At the same time, though, you had to be careful around him if you had anything to protect. Either money or a pedigree, or something real behind those things. Ted was part of the hungry world, the world that always wants the surface stuff and doesn't care what it damages getting to it. Ted didn't know there was anything behind money and birth and didn't want to know. So you had to be careful around him, because without realizing it, he was dangerous for you on all counts.

He wasn't alone. The world is full of people like Ted, and you have to be careful around all of them. What you really have to watch out for is you yourself acting out their idea of you, what Arabella had done. They don't want to hurt you, they just want you to be their idea of you so they can watch it, like a play. If you fall for that and act for them, you'll ruin yourself, but it won't be their fault. They'll be sorry afterward that you've fallen apart, but they won't know how it happened. They'll think you just fell apart on your own, without a clue that it had anything to do with them.

Anyhow, Arabella had fallen into the trap and been pathetic with him, and now she wasn't. And even when she had been pathetic, she'd had so much spirit that it was the spirit and not the being pathetic that really mattered.

She smiled at me while I was finishing up quite a bit of Carmen's roast beef, and rolled her eyes toward the end of the dining room, toward the painting called *Hunting the Hunters*. I couldn't remember if I'd told her about it, but it was a good backdrop to what was going on.

Then we stopped teasing Ted, and just had a good time for the rest of the meal.

After dinner I went upstairs to my room, and Arabella followed along in about fifteen minutes. I was lying on my bed and she sat on the foot of it.

"How are you?" she asked me. "You look fine."

"I'm all right."

"No one paid any attention to your wounds, poor dear, or even asked after your health."

"Better that way."

"The way you ate, though—you've got to be all right."

"I think so."

"I've never seen anyone put it away like that."

"I can do better."

"Didn't mean to be personal—sorry."

"I don't mind."

"Your father isn't bad."

"How well do you know him?"

"Not at all. . . . We talked before dinner."

"I know."

"He was nice enough. Looks *just* like Tom Buchanan, by the way—at least my idea of Tom Buchanan. Except that he's better-looking."

"Tell him that?"

"Of course not. Sally's all right, too. She's loaning me a nightie."

Then she said, "I'm so ashamed of having a father like Andy Candy."

"Don't be."

"He's so awful."

"He doesn't even seem related to you. Doesn't look a bit like you."

"I always have done that kid thing of not believing he's my father."

"Don't worry about it. I've done the same thing myself. I used to think my grandfather was my father, with no mother at all. Everyone does it one way or another. Forget it."

"All right." She was quiet again. Then she said, "Big day—super slugfest."

"You're on it there."

"You got my note?"

"Sure."

"Like it?"

"Very much."

"Mean that?"

"Of course."

"I wanted to know—I do so many things badly."

"Not letters—you're unbeatable there."

"Lots of other things."

"Not so many."

"Lots."

"Less than you think."

She didn't say anything, but looked at me, her face very simple and straight.

"What about dinner tonight?"

"What about it?"

"I made a fool of myself, chattering away at Ted."

I didn't say anything.

"Didn't I?"

"You know you did."

"If Sally hadn't stepped in, I don't know how long I would have gone on. When I do that . . . it's what I call having a mouth like a watermelon. It's disgusting."

"You mean you know you're doing it?"

"Oh, sure."

"And you still do it?"

"Over and over."

"And you can't stop?"

"Can't seem to. I tell myself I'll beat it next time, but I never do. It's called compulsion. I'm compulsive—added to everything else. Or it's all part of the same thing. But let's not go into that."

"I didn't, you did."

"Yes, well, let's not."

She was in sort of a bad mood suddenly, and I kept quiet, to let her work it out.

After a while, she smiled at me. "I'm sorry, Ox, of all people I shouldn't be short with you."

"I don't mind," I said. I didn't, either.

She put her hand over mine. "I told Sally I was grateful to her for what she did tonight. But I could never tell you how grateful I am to you. It's beyond gratitude."

"Let's not get heavy," I said, kidding her a little.

"You know what I mean," she said.

"I know what you mean," I said.

"You were kidding me."

"I was kidding you."

"I'd kiss you good night if you wouldn't think I was forward," she said. "But what am I saying? You don't make mistakes like that."

She leaned forward and kissed me on the cheek. Her lips were warm and calm.

Then she got up, smoothed her skirt, and went to the door.

"Good night, Achilles," she said in a different voice,

having fun for both of us. "I can't tell you what it means to a poor waif like meself to be sleeping under the same roof with yourself." She was working on an Irish accent, and it wasn't bad. "Or should I be saying under the same roof with himself? Begorrah, when you feel like this, it's not knowing what you're saying that you are . . . "

She dropped it then and said, "Good night, Ox," with her face very simple and straight again, and went out, closing the door softly behind her.

I switched out the light and lay there in the darkness, too lazy to undress and get into bed. The stitches hurt a little, and I could feel the bandage pressing.

I lay there for a couple of hours like that, not in any hurry to get to sleep. If I'd wanted to, I could have taken a sedative and a painkiller that the doctor had given me. Except that I had a lot to think about, and I wanted to take my time doing it. But even with all the time in the world, I guess there are some things you can't think through. You can figure out why something happened, or what someone meant, or what you should do about something, but it's very hard to work out what you yourself actually feel. It should be the easiest, because it's you alone with yourself, but it's the hardest.

14

WHEN I WOKE UP NEXT MORNING, Hans was shaking me.

"You were coming downstairs down," he said. "Your father wanted you."

"What time is it?"

"It was eight."

"Hans, I don't get up at eight."

"You was, this morning. Your father was saying no excuses. Someone was with him."

"Who?"

"I was not telling you. Maybe then your curiosity was making you get up."

"I'm an invalid, I . . ."

"No excuses. Sorry. How was the head?"

"Terrible." It wasn't, but there was no point in saying so.

"Ox, you was sleeping in your clothes!"

"Only some of them."

"That was awful. Wait a minute." He rubbed his fat stomach and looked worried. He had a soft spot for animals and people who were sick. "Maybe I was telling your father you were not well enough to get up. Maybe?"

"I can make it." I knew anything was better than getting Dad sore.

So I pulled a robe over the general mess and went downstairs, and then down again into the sunken living room, and there was Dad with an old man I'd never seen before.

"Ox, this is Mr. Revere," Dad said, and Mr. Revere got up to shake hands with me.

"I hope you feel all right," he said.

He was about seventy-five, but in very good shape, a tall, thin, handsome old man, with a pleasant voice and kind eyes. I liked him right away, and wondered how he'd gotten himself married to Lizzie.

"Well, I can walk," I said. Even though I liked him, I didn't want to give too much away.

"I'm sorry about what happened yesterday," he said. "And last night, as well. I've come to talk to your father—and to you—to see if we can't put things right."

We found out later that when Mr. Revere had come home the night before and found out that I—a minor—had been hit with a shovel, he had told Lizzie *she* was in trouble because the law and the newspapers would take my side. She argued with him, and they finally called her lawyers, who said Mr. Revere was right. By that time she'd already sent Big Andy off, all steamed up, and it was too late to call him back—I guess it was just about then that he was being flattened. Then when he showed up with more trouble, in which he was in the wrong, Mr. Revere said there was nothing to do but for him to come over to Severn House early the next day and settle it on the best terms he could. Lizzie was wild, but there was nothing she could do. The maids had heard it all, and they talked and it all came floating back through Hans.

"I hope we can straighten it out," Dad said to Mr. Revere, deadpan, "but these are serious matters. Ox could have been killed. So could I, for that matter."

"Well, um, I grant you that Ox was attacked . . . in an, um, unwarranted fashion. But in your case, Andy—um, Big Andy—says he was slugged for no reason. Anyhow, there are no marks on you, Mr. Olmstead, and Big Andy looks awful. So I'll give you Ox, but not yourself."

He said it so pleasantly, and with such a feeling for everything, that Dad had to grin.

"All right," Dad said, "we'll leave Big Andy out of it— at least for the moment. Now what about the attack on Ox? What does your concession about that mean?"

"Well, what does it mean?" Mr. Revere asked bluntly. "I suppose you're entitled to some damages, if you want to get right down to it. But you're not a poor man, so what good would a few extra dollars do you? I'll write you out a check for five thousand right now if you want it. That's probably all a court would give you."

"You're right, no point in that chicken feed," Dad said. "But . . . "

"Let me finish, please," Mr. Revere said. "Then you could press charges against Jack Taffle, but what's the point in putting a poor man in jail?"

"None," Dad said. "He was only carrying out orders."

"That's arguable," Mr. Revere said. "When you get to the end, what's left except an apology, and I'm giving you that."

"But are you the person to give the apology?" Dad asked him.

"Why aren't I? It happened on my wife's property."

"Exactly. Her property, not yours. And she was standing there, egging this Taffle on. He wouldn't have done it if she hadn't been there. She's responsible, not you, and I want to settle it with her."

"That's impossible," Mr. Revere said in a short way.

"Why?"

"Mrs. Revere doesn't get involved in this sort of thing."

"She got involved enough to damn nearly have Ox killed."

"That's not true." Mr. Revere was starting to get red in the face.

"Of course it's true. She was right there and she had it done."

Mr. Revere stood up. "I came here to settle this man-to-man. But evidently all you're interested in doing is picking on a woman. I didn't realize you were so ungentlemanly."

It was the wrong thing to say to Dad.

"I didn't know that a man who lives off an old woman is in a position to define what a gentleman does or doesn't do," he said with a nasty grin.

It took Mr. Revere a moment to get it. Then he went white and began to say something, but changed his mind and started out.

Dad and I watched him go. When we heard the front door slam, Dad shrugged and said, "Poor old booby."

I didn't say anything.

"I suppose you think I was too tough."

"I didn't say that."

"I can feel you thinking it."

"Then you're wrong. I think you did it just right."

"Pulling my leg?"

"No, I'm being honest. He was all right up to a point, but then he broke down on what she had a right to do. He's like the rest, thinks she's some kind of god."

"That's it, all right, and that's what I can't eat. But I didn't know you cared about things like that. I mean, I thought that like all kids today you figure everything in the adult world is the same, and to hell with it."

"No, there are differences and I try to pay attention to them."

"Do you think most kids do?"

"No."

"Why not? If you do, why don't they?"

"I don't know . . . maybe they've got less to protect."

"You mean money? Why, Ox, I never knew you cared."

"No, I don't mean money."

"What do you mean?"

"Something else, something more important than money."

"*What,* for Christ's sake?"

"I can't put it in words, but it's got something to do with what you are."

"And what are you?"

"I'm not sure. I'm too young to know that."

"Such modesty," Dad said with a grin. "Seriously, though, I didn't know you were such a deep thinker."

"That's not so deep."

"Anybody who thinks anything is more important than money is deep," Dad said. "Everyone pretends to, but no one does. Very, very few, anyhow."

"You did yourself, a minute ago," I said. "It wasn't

money that made you give it to Mr. Revere. It was personal."

He stared at me. "My God, Ox, what are you? Some kind of psychiatrist? No, I'm only kidding. You're right—I was doing it for myself. I've always taken care of myself, my own pride, whatever they call it. And I'll tell you something else, just to close this little heart-to-heart out. I've always known that you were one of those very, very few for whom money wasn't everything. Especially protecting money. Now go up and get dressed right—that robe should be burned—and get going on whatever it is that you have to do, before we start telling each other all our secrets."

It was the first sort of compliment he had ever paid me. And the first time we'd ever had any kind of halfway real talk. I didn't know what it meant. I did know it didn't necessarily mean we'd ever have another one. We might—but we might not, either.

15

AFTER I GOT DRESSED I went down to the kitchen, and Carmen really went to work.

"Waffles and sausages," she said. "I think a little breakfast steak, too."

"That sounds about right," I said.

"You're up early this morning. Is there anything wrong? Oh, I forget—Hans told me—you had to go down and see your father and Mr. Revere. It was surely OK?" She looked at me anxiously, wanting to be sure I hadn't suffered.

"It was fine, Carmen."

"And the head is all right?"

"Fine."

She went back to work, and while I was waiting Dad came through on his way to the city.

"I don't know what the next act will be," he said, "but Arabella better go back today."

"She won't want to."

"She can't stay here. They'll have me up for kidnapping. If she can't stand it there, you can give her enough to hide out somewhere else."

"I don't have any money."

He looked around to make sure Carmen wouldn't hear. "I'll give it to you. Here's five hundred for a starter. Just don't let it ever get traced back to me."

"What if it gets traced back to me?"

"You're the knight in shining armor, aren't you? You don't care." He grinned at me. "And don't tell her where it came from. Got it?"

"All right."

"If you're smart, you'll tell her to keep your name out of it, too. Incidentally, that money is for only one purpose. Don't blow it anywhere else. And if she doesn't want to hide out, I expect it back."

"Talk about wanting it all ways."

"Isn't it awful." He looked at his watch. "Chopper's due in five minutes. By the way, what was all that about 'When you see her, you'll know she's not the kind of girl anyone sneaks over to see.' I think she's devastating."

"I didn't mean she isn't attractive. I meant she isn't someone you sneak around with."

"What would you know about that? Well, don't tell me. Anyhow, devastating, but plenty of trouble, I'll guarantee that. See you." And he zoomed out the back door.

I was stuffing the money in my pants when Sally came out. She asked me how I felt, but she didn't say anything about how early it was for me to be up. Sally was always good that way.

"Pretty fair," I said. "Say, where does Dad meet the helicopter?"

"At that field down at the end of the property. You can hear it when it comes. He gave me the word on Arabella—it's too bad, but there's no other way. Yes," she said, reading my eyes, "he told me about the financial arrangements. Don't worry, I can keep my mouth shut. Especially when I'm more or less off the stuff."

"You look a lot better, off," I said. She did, too.

"Flattery will get you nowhere," she said automatically. "Listen, before Arabella shows up, I want to tell you I like her. I didn't at first, and I still don't know if she's all there, but I like her. She has a certain something. And she's well mannered."

"Flattery will get you nowhere," I said.

Sally laughed. "Ah, Ox, you're the one," she said. "Listen, if there are any attacks from the Revere camp today, I'm supposed to handle them, with your muscle and brain backing me up. Arabella has to be out by sundown, but until then we keep her under cover and don't produce her."

"What if they arrive with cops and court orders?"

"Barry says they can't get them that fast. Besides, after this morning, they'll have to go back for another round with their lawyers. Last item—you give the word to Arabella."

"Naturally."

"Well, you're . . . Ox, she really respects you."

"There's no accounting for taste."

"Don't you ever let down?"

"Only with my enemies."

"This is getting too fast for me," she said. "See you later. Say—do you want to drive over to Manhasset this afternoon with Arabella? There's a lamp that needs picking up." She cocked her head. "That's the helicopter now. Hear it?"

I did—it sounded the way a helicopter was supposed to.

I said I'd get the lamp, and then I said, "I want to thank you for yesterday—for everything you did."

"Just taking a casualty to the hospital, nothing at all."

"You did more than that. Last night at dinner, you know what you did."

"I didn't think you noticed skirmishes in the social game."

"How could anyone miss it?"

"It's nice of you to say so, anyhow. You're always nice, Ox. Women appreciate that, more than you may realize."

"I'm only nice to nice women."

"And they'll always love you for it. All nice women are the same, really, and you'll always have the same effect on them."

She said it lightly, but I could tell it was important to her that she tell me that.

Then she left and I buckled down to breakfast. It was extra large, even by Carmen's standards, and she watched me put it away like some sort of religious person in front of an altar. Ted came in toward the end, and made a noise about how early I was up, and how that meant we could really have a big day at the books.

"You're not serious," I said. "You don't think an accident victim—one with a *head* injury—is ready for study the day after it happens, do you?"

"You're well enough to eat this outsize breakfast."

"That's to build up my strength," I told him. "That has nothing to do with brain damage."

"I think you're well enough to work," he said. There was a little edge in his voice that had never been there before. I thought it might have been caused by the night before, after he thought it over.

"I'm telling you I'm not," I told him, "so forget it." I gave him the edge right back. It was the first time I'd ever done that, but it was his first, too.

"You can't talk to me that way," he said.

"I just did it."

"Then . . . you'd better not do it again."

"Then stop acting that way."

"Acting what way?"

"Like an hysterical woman."

His mouth popped open. "Hysterical woman? What do you know about . . . ?" He looked around, trying to find someone to agree with him that . . . well, he wasn't sure, but it covered a lot of ground, including women's lib. When he found he was all alone—Carmen was no help, especially with women's lib—he swung back, all ready to start in again.

"Wait a minute," I said. "Before you say something you may regret, just take ten."

"You are the cheekiest . . . how could I regret . . . ?" He'd started to stutter and had to take ten after all to get it under control.

"You could work yourself up to the point where you'd get so excited you'd quit your job. That's OK if that's the way you want it, but not if you don't."

He looked at me a long time. "You know, you really are an arrogant bastard under all that calm indifference! You're a typical rich boy after all, aren't you. It took me a long time to figure it out, but . . . "

"If you want to go on howling, go do it somewhere else."

"You can't tell me where to go."

"Can't I? Listen, I don't mind when you kid me, and I don't mind when you lecture me. Because there's no meanness in it. But when you come in here feeling sore about something and try to take it out on me, then I fight back. Especially at breakfast! Don't take out your own troubles on me, and especially not when I'm eating!"

I figured the only way to shut him up was to make more noise than he did, and I was really yelling at the end. But it worked. He swallowed hard, and backed away from the table, and went and got a glass of water and paced up and down for a minute. Carmen was watching it all, and winked at me.

"I certainly didn't mean to 'take out my troubles' on you, Ox," he finally said. His voice was calm, which was good, but I was afraid he was going to make a speech, which was bad.

"I wasn't aware that I had any troubles," he went on, and then he did make a speech, all about how he had always tried to be fair, and he wouldn't dream of getting confused and taking out his troubles on someone else and not knowing it. He went on and on, and I let him go, because all he was doing was putting himself back together and he had to do that or he couldn't go on. When he got all done, he'd be the same old Ted, but there'd be a memory of what had happened, and he wouldn't do it again. I wasn't sorry I'd let him have it, because what I said was true—he was taking out his troubles on me, and no one has to put up with that, especially at breakfast—but on the other hand, he was such an amateur in being mean that you had to let him pull himself together.

When he was all finished, he stopped and put his hand out and said, "Now can we be friends again?"

"Sure," I said, and we shook on it.

"You are an arrogant rich boy, though," he said. "I'll

stick on that." But he said it with a smile and there was no edge in his voice.

"I never pretend to be anything else," I said.

He thought about that, and then he sat down and had a cup of coffee and was his old self again. There was no more talk about my working, except as a way of getting at what had been on his mind all along.

"Forget about studying today," he said. "And tomorrow, too. Say, that reminds me, what about Arabella? Is she going to stay on here and study with us?"

"I don't know. Do you think that would be a good idea?"

"Oh, I do. She's such an intelligent girl. It would raise the whole level of . . . our classroom. I don't mean to say that you're not a . . . challenge for any teacher yourself, Ox, but it's always easier to work with two. . . . So I hope she'll be able to stay."

"She's kind of talkative, though."

"Yes, well, you mean like last night. But some of what she was saying was brilliant. She lives in a real fantasy world." Ted went for *Peanuts* and the Hobbits and *Watership Down* and anything else like that. "Fantasy" meant "good." He didn't realize that Arabella's valley was very different from that other stuff.

"I don't know," I said. "If she were better looking . . . "

"Why, she's beautiful," Ted burst out. "I mean, for a girl her age. She doesn't have *Playboy* looks, I'll grant you, if that's what you're after, and I suppose you are, but she has . . . a kind of timeless beauty."

He sort of bit his tongue after he said that, because he knew it sounded sappy. He looked at me to see how I was taking it, and I was deadpan.

I only said, "That sounds pretty good."

Because I wasn't laughing at him, he said, "She reminds me of Katharine Hepburn—you never saw her when she was young, but she was something."

"You're not old enough to have seen her then yourself, are you?"

"I've seen her in old films," he said.

"Anybody can see anybody in an old film. Me as well as you."

"Well . . . I didn't think you'd like that sort of film. Too 'intellectual,' or 'civilized.' Like *The Philadelphia Story.*"

"I saw it," I said.

"Like it?"

"It was all right. But Arabella doesn't remind me of Katharine Hepburn—she's more like Carol Burnett."

"Carol Burnett? Are you crazy? Why, Carol Burnett isn't . . . she's witty, I guess, if you can stand the repetition, but her looks, she . . . no, Arabella is really attractive. And has so much breeding in her face. You can see it in her bone structure."

"What's this? Arabella the great beauty?" It was Arabella herself, she'd come in without Ted seeing her.

"Oh, I'm so sorry," he said, scrambling up. "I didn't mean . . . "

"And Carol Burnett? She looks just like the British royal family—the Queen and Anne and Charles, especially—Hanoverian horse-heavy in the face—although Carol jumps around more than they do. Maybe she's a relative—born on the wrong side of the horse blanket or something."

Ted just gaped at her.

"Ted says you look like Katharine Hepburn," Carmen crowed.

"I didn't mean . . . " Ted began.

"That's so sweet of you," Arabella said. "Although it's not a bit true. I really look like Joan Crawford."

She knew how to handle him now.

"I thought that perhaps you might like to look over some of our books if you're going to be here . . . " he began.

She shot a quick look at me.

"We have to go to Manhasset to get a lamp," I said.

"It will only take a minute," Ted said.

"That's awfully kind of you, Ted, but I have some things to do before we go."

He made another try before he gave up. Then he wouldn't get out of the kitchen, so we had to. I went first and Arabella followed me.

Up in my room, she said, "What's all this about Manhasset?"

"Sally said there was a lamp to get there, and she thought you and I might like to drive over."

"Sounds fine. When do we go?"

"I was thinking about this afternoon, but with Ted prowling around I guess we might as well go now."

"All right. Ox, what happened this morning when Martin was here?"

"Martin?"

"Martin Revere."

"I'll tell you on the way."

"And what's going to become of me?"

"Tell you that on the way, too."

"All right." She seemed calm. "What was all that about Carol Burnett?"

"I was teasing Ted. He's crazy about you."

"Well, Arabella—or Carol, or Joan—can't say she's too flattered. Is he always that stupid?"

"He's worse around you."

"Cut it out. You know, we could have a time with him if I joined you in the classroom."

"We could."

"Are we going to?"

"We'll talk about that on the way. Now get ready."

"I don't get to stay, do I?" She was calm, but she was hurting.

"See you downstairs."

We were on our way into the garage when Hans spotted us.

"You were not driving, Ox," he said. "Not with that head injury like that. No, I was driving you. Where were you going?"

I argued that I was all right, but he wouldn't let go.

"Then Arabella can drive," I said.

"No license," she said.

"Why not?"

"Can't get one in New York State until you're eighteen. It's not like Florida."

So Hans drove us after all. Only he didn't drive us to Manhasset. At the last minute, Sally came down into the garage and said the lamp didn't matter. "If you're going to have an outing, why not go into the city. Have lunch, and Hans can drive you back."

"I'd love that," Arabella said gratefully. Then she said, "But I can't go in these clothes."

"You're too big for any of mine," Sally said. "And you wouldn't like them anyhow."

"Don't be too sure," Arabella said. "Miss Gunnysacks

is grateful for anything. Listen," she said to me, "I can slip over to my house and change. I know how to get in and out without anyone seeing me. You and Hans go around and park near the main drive—I'll meet you there in half an hour."

We told her it was dangerous, but she wasn't going to the city in what she had on from the afternoon before. So off she went.

I didn't think it would work, but it did. Hans and I timed it to a half hour, and we were barely parked a couple of hundred yards from the entrance to Myrtle Grove when out she came. She had on a coat that buttoned right up to the neck and high-heeled shoes and gloves. Her long hair was full of shine, and she looked very much dressed for the city. I had put on a tie, but the rest was fairly sloppy, and the bandage finished it off. We weren't a match.

We were using the leased limousine, which Dad still had, even though he didn't take it to the city anymore. You could put the partition window up and shut off the chauffeur, which Hans didn't like, because he always wanted to talk, but I told him it made a breeze on my head.

It was an enormous car, with a bar and television and telephone, and when you pushed the jump seats up in back you had as much space as if you were in a small room.

"You could live in this thing," Arabella said as she got in.

"Any trouble?"

"None. My mother was in the house, but I got by her. Both ways. Leave it to Arabella."

We were rolling down the country roads leading to the Long Island Expressway, and it was a beautiful day. But cold, the weather had definitely changed now and it was winter, not like it had been. I lay back in my seat and looked out and thought that a lot of people would do almost anything to be where I was, mainly people who thought money solved everything.

"Let's call somewhere on that phone," Arabella said. "Somewhere far away, like Buenos Aires."

The name triggered something, and I remembered that Mom had said she was going there. Her latest comic card had been from Lima, she was working her way by stages.

"Why Buenos Aires? Do you know anyone there?"

"No, just sounded far away. Do you?"

"In a way." Then I remembered that Hans and Carmen were from there. Or had stopped there on the way from Germany. And thinking of them made me think of food, and that made me ask Arabella, "Did you get any breakfast this morning?"

"No."

"I just figured out you couldn't have, because you came down after I did. We'll stop and . . . "

"No, I don't need any. I never eat breakfast."

"You never eat breakfast?" I couldn't believe it. "Why, that's the cause of all your troubles, Arabella. That explains everything."

Just the idea of what her stomach went through every morning had my own in instant agony.

16

I TRIED TO TALK TO HER about how necessary it is to have a good breakfast, how all the health experts say that, but she couldn't see it.

"You're only making excuses for your own phenomenal eating," she said with a laugh.

I kept at it, and she told me she was never hungry in the morning. I said that was hard to believe—everyone is hungry in the morning, even if it's only a little.

Her face got hard and set, and she said, "After I had anorexia, they tried to make me eat all the time. It was like stuffing a goose. I went the other way and got too fat, and had a hard time taking it off. Now I can't stand it if anyone tries to push me at food, even you, Ox. So leave me alone on it. I know what I'm doing."

I said OK, and dropped it.

It had sort of spoiled our trip and we were both quiet, looking out the windows on each side.

It was a landscape to remember, and I thought about it to take my mind off our food talk. Long Island is about the worst I've ever seen for pollution and noise and cars and inconvenience and ugliness, and it isn't even warm like Los Angeles to make up for it. There are other places in America as ugly, lots and lots of them—most of them, I guess—but Long Island takes the cake. It's useless in a way all its own. Especially as Christmas closes in, and the pathetic trimmings float around in the general mess.

I was thinking along like that, and Arabella touched my hand and said, "I'm sorry."

"That's all right. It was my fault."

"No, it was mine. Let's not go into it, let's drop it. What were you going to tell me?"

"Dad says you can't stay because he'd be liable for harboring you. I can't say he's wrong."

"I knew that. I don't blame him."

"Wait a minute. There's another possibility. I have money . . . "

"I know you have money," she said, batting her eyes slightly.

"Be serious. I have enough money to stake you if you want to go somewhere on your own."

"You mean run away?"

"That's it."

She thought it over, sitting up straight and holding her gloves in her lap. "What do you do when you run away? No, I'm serious. What do you do? Hitchhike up and down the country? I don't want to do that. Become a whore? Don't want that, either. Get mugged? Probably. Raped? Almost certainly. Not a pretty picture."

"What if you just holed up somewhere? Even in Manhattan, so you wouldn't be too far away."

"Do you know what that would cost?"

"How much?"

"A decent small apartment costs four hundred. Living, another three. Then three for emergencies. Say a thousand a month."

"I think I could come up with that."

"Say, mister, how rich *are* you?" She was laughing. "There are certified playboys on the North Shore who can't come up with that kind of money, and here you are . . . a seventeen-year-old with . . . ah, Ox, you're wonderful!" She leaned over and kissed me, and her lips were fresh and warm. "You're wonderful," she repeated.

"I'm just rich," I said. I was supposed to be, because Dad was, but of course I never saw much actual cash. Poor kids had a lot more go through their hands than I did. Arabella knew that rich kids could never come up with money in any quantity, but she probably figured the Olmsteads were so different about everything—why not money, too?

"You're setting me up in a love nest!" she crowed. " 'Teenager's Mistress in Sutton Place Hideaway—read all about it!' I want to do it—it's the only thing that's ever happened to me. My big chance. I'll be a great mistress, I promise. What do they do? I mean, besides you-know-what. Sew on buttons? Cook? I'm no Carmen, I'm not even one-eighth of a Carmen. By the way, someone should sew up her uniforms for her. I can't boil water. How will I feed you? To say nothing of the other . . . and I'm so skinny. How can I make it as a mistress? Aren't they supposed to be curvy and . . . "

"Come on, this is serious."

"But . . . "

"Shut up. You don't want to go back to your own house, and you can't stay with us. The only possibility is staying with relatives or friends . . . "

"Uh-uh." She shook her head.

" . . . or being on your own. Relatives are out because they'll turn you back in. Friends . . . do you have any?"

"Are you kidding? Do you?"

"I have a few." I was thinking of the Lattimores in Philadelphia, and Dale Tifton, and a few others. But if the Waterlukkers found her with any of those people—and they could mount a real search—then my friends would be in trouble, and it would come back to me, and to Dad. "But they're not right for this, with the connection to me."

"You're clever. Just like a gangster."

"Cut it out. The only solution is for you to live on your own. I'll keep the money coming to you." I knew Dad would go through with that. A thousand a month was nothing to him—even if it lasted a year, it was only twelve—and he had committed himself. "Just remember—if they find you, you have to keep my name out of it. Especially about where you got the money."

"Coward—and just when I thought you were so brave, being my protector and all."

"I don't mind trouble, but I don't like trouble where I have to lose. Financing you leaves me wide open to anything if they find out. And gets Dad on my back. I don't want it."

"I understand . . . but what about me?"

"You mean if they find you?"

"That's what I mean."

"They can yell, but they don't have you in a legal bind, the way they would anyone who helped you."

"I see . . . yes, that's right. Now let me think about it seriously for a minute."

She thought and I stared out the window. We were

143

passing the highrise apartments near Queens Boulevard, just about the low point on the whole trip.

Hans caught my eye in the mirror and signaled that he wanted to say something. I switched on the intercom, and he said, "I was rather being dead than living here." He nodded his head several times. "I was meaning that!"

"I guess that's the way we were all feeling," I said and switched off.

"He's not so dumb," Arabella said, "even if he does put his feet in the soup."

"How did you know?"

"Hans is famous," she said. "Everyone in Locust Valley knows Hans. Or knows about him. I've seen him around since I can remember. Put him under a bridge in the valley, first-class mean little troll. But I'd never seen him in action until last night and today. You people can really come up with the servants."

"We inherited them."

She was looking out at the apartments. "Why send the beautiful people to the mountains? Why not put them all in these cozy little flats? Can't you see Jackie O. in one of them, cooking for twenty relatives and trying to unplug the sink at the same time? She . . . "

"Have you been thinking about what you were supposed to be thinking about?"

"Ox, I don't think I can do it," she said sadly.

"That's too bad."

"Listen, don't have contempt for me. My problem is loneliness. That's why I got anorexia in the first place. I can't be alone. I know it. Even Andy Candy and my poor mother and the people at Myrtle Grove are some-

thing, if only to fight with. But to be alone in this city . . .
I couldn't do it."

"I'd come and see you."

"Once a week."

"Maybe twice. Maybe even three times."

"For how many hours? No, I'd be alone ninety percent of the time. I couldn't stand it. But before you give
up on me, remember that not many girls could, anorexia or no anorexia."

"I don't blame you."

"Yes, you do, you think I'm so weak, that any other
girl would be able to do it. But . . . "

"I know it's not easy. It wouldn't be easy for me. I
don't know if I could do it."

"You could do it. For one thing, you're a man. Well,
you're supposed to be a boy, but you're really a man
because . . . you're so big, and other reasons we won't go
into here. You can move around in this city, or anywhere. There are so many more things you can do on
your own. And you know how to make yourself comfortable with people. I'm such . . . an eccentric. I can't
get along with people the way you do."

"Yes, I'm great at that," I said.

"Well, you are, in a way."

We swung clear of the Brooklyn-Queens Expressway
and the traffic cleared out and all the skyscrapers in
Manhattan were coming at us.

"The city of dreams," Arabella said softly.

"Only none of them ever come true."

"Depends on what you're dreaming about. Listen,
I've just had an idea! Do you really have a lot of money?
I mean, on you, right now?"

"A fair amount."

"Then let's go to some hotel and have a big lunch for you and a carrot or something for me. Then you go out, and I sit around and *see* if I can take it. Then you drop back in a few hours, just the way you might be dropping in, and we'll settle it then."

"That's a terrible idea." Her shining face fell. "No, it's really a wonderful idea—can't you ever tell when you're being kidded?"

"No. Especially not by you."

"Got any ideas about hotels?"

"Not any good ones. There aren't any good hotels anymore, anyhow . . . what am I doing with all those any's? So there's no point in pretending with the Plaza or the Pierre. Never mind, a really bad one can be fun . . . what about the Morville?"

"Sounds right."

"I can't wait. How do we get rid of Hans?"

"Easy. Where is the Morville?"

"Park, about Fifty-fifth."

I picked up the intercom and got him. "Hans, drop us at Park and Fifty-third."

"What you were doing there?" he asked in his suspicious way.

"They're having a big lamp show in that neighborhood today. Sally asked us to look in on it."

"She was saying lamps were not to be important—that's why we were not to Manhasset going," Hans said. "How come we now were going for lamps in Manhattan?"

We were coming up to the tunnel and I said, "There isn't time to argue, Hans. Just drop us there."

"Where I was meeting you to take you back?"

"You aren't. We'll take the train."

He started to argue again, and I switched it off.

"That's a handy gadget," Arabella said.

Just before the tunnel, one of those young Americans who dress up like Oriental monks was fixing a flat on his car, which was pulled off to the side. They wear sandals and some thin orange gowns wrapped around them, and shave their heads except for a sort of scalp lock. All Oriental, except for the same old American faces hanging out in front. You see them all over Manhattan. They beat little drums and chant and try to talk about religion to people passing by. I never thought of any of them as being involved with a car.

Arabella saw him, too, and smiled at me. "They have to get into town like everybody else," she said.

When Hans dropped us, he wanted to go over it again. "I was responsible for you. What was your father saying tonight? What train you were taking back?"

"Forget it," I said. "We'll get back all right, don't worry." I was outside the car and conscious of people staring at it and me. "See you later."

We strolled off, and the staring didn't stop.

"That bandage atop your bulk has the natives going," Arabella murmured, her eyes straight ahead. She had her gloves on now, and looked wonderful in the cold. And from a different time, too.

"They're looking at you," I told her. "Turning around."

"Don't kid me, I can't compare with . . . what's next to me. I'm only a socialite—you're an aristocrat."

"What's the difference?"

"Socialites are herd animals, cowardly. Aristocrats stand alone."

"You're not a herd animal."

"Yes, I am, especially in a pinch. I'd like not to be, more than anything, but I haven't made it—I may never. You've always been there."

"Now who's kidding?"

She laughed cheerfully. "Not me, you're the real thing."

"That's what Helen Hayes says about Linda Lovelace, isn't it?"

She laughed again, and said something about me proving her point by saying that, but the wind was blowing and I didn't catch it all.

When we got to the Morville, we stopped just inside to check signals.

Arabella smiled up at me. "If I live to be a thousand, I'll never forget you," she said. "Do you know that?"

I felt something I'd never felt before for anyone. I thought it was because I liked her so much and was so sorry for her, but I know now it was something else.

"Can't dawdle here," she said. "Let's get that room. Who'll do it?"

"I will."

"You don't think the bandage will frighten them?"

"Everything is so crazy these days—they'll just think I'm a personality who's had a bad night—a rock star, probably. . . . Arabella, I didn't answer you a moment ago because I didn't think it was a question."

"It wasn't. I just wanted you to know."

"It's not a small thing to know," I told her, moving off to the desk.

There was no trouble—I was Franklin Olmstead and I paid one hundred and eight dollars for a room with a sitting room and a few other extras. Arabella was standing next to me, and when the clerk sort of glanced at her, I said, "She's a singer with The Klondike." He didn't want to be so stupid as not to know what group The Klondike was, so he just nodded and that was that.

17

UP IN THE SUITE, Arabella threw herself on
the big bed and laughed. "Is there a group called The
Klondike?"

"I don't know."

"You mean you invented it?"

"I thought it up to go with the rock star, just to have it
ready." I'd known a horse once called Klondike, and
that was how the name came to me.

"They never asked for luggage or anything. If you
could have seen the assistant manager peeking around
the corner, and the rest of the lobby . . . Gargantua with
his bandage." She laughed into the pillow.

It was still only about eleven, too early to order lunch,
so we kicked off our shoes and talked. Before we settled
down, Arabella hung her coat up neatly and laid her
gloves out on a table. She was very precise about things
like that.

Arabella told me a lot that day. To start with, she told
me all about old Mr. Revere. How Lizzie Waterlukker
had had two husbands before, but neither one of them

turned out the way she wanted. The first one was a businessman of some kind, and she'd had a couple of kids with him. They were grown now and had kids of their own. Then he said the wrong thing at dinner or something, and she divorced him. After that she married a doctor, but he didn't last long. He crossed her one day about the color of the new curtains and that was all for him. Finally, Revere, who was a banker. All of them were respectable, and had a little money—Revere even had a million or two of his own—but she didn't fool around with anyone who was anywhere near her financial league.

"They've all been stick figures for her," Arabella said. "She comes on like . . . like a great actress who has all sorts of requirements. Up at such and such an hour. Toast just so at breakfast, room temperature at a certain tenth of a degree, ditto bath. 'Isn't there a draft?' So many rules and regulations. Of course, she doesn't care about that stuff—it's just to keep them running. And they never ask themselves what it's all for, or why she's so important. They just accept it. Martin Revere is really a sweet old man, except on the subject of her."

She told me how he worked on the staff to keep the air conditioners just right, and all the household noises down, and the car springs from squeaking. "Noises no one else can hear. She even got him to call a neighbor one day to complain about a chain saw going three miles away. Barely a hum on the summer air. The neighbor— Pat Hopkins—told Martin to shove it, and the poor old fool wanted to fight a duel with him. 'Mrs. Revere is trying to take her nap. How can you be so heartless? I'll come over and turn it off myself.' It's pathetic."

We started talking about other kids and she said she never met any she liked.

"Maybe they're better in Palm Beach, but here the boys are so stupid you think they're retarded. Everything so slowed down, too. 'Did . . . you . . . go . . . to . . . Bar Harbor . . . last . . . summer?' 'Do . . . you . . . know . . . the . . . Fishers?' 'Are . . . you . . . going . . . to . . . college?' 'Say . . . that's . . . real . . . keen.' And all the girls I know play right back to it—actually, I'm being too kind, because they're that way themselves. They *all* think I'm nuts. Not only because of what I say, but because I can get out more than two words a minute and my voice has inflections instead of the fashionable monotone. They're so boring—and they must be the same in Palm Beach. And coast to coast. Don't they bore you?"

"Yes, but I try not to pay any attention to them."

"So clever of you. But listen, Ox, isn't it strange that everyone our age is a zombie?"

"I guess so."

"You'd think the newspapers would be full of it. Biggest story of the age. But they aren't. Why?"

"People can't face it."

"I suppose so. And they're not slowed down because they want to be, the way all their parents think. They're slowed down, period. And then they try to figure out how to live with it. Something happened to them, they're retarded. It must have been the food they ate. And eat. All those poisons. And the air . . . " She gestured crisply toward the outdoors. "But why didn't it happen to you and me? Why are we different? The way kids used to be, maybe? Not exactly, but more that way?

152

Why? Did we eat differently? Say, we did, at that. I didn't eat at all, and you ate too much . . . "

Later she talked about the magic valley.

"I always knew there had to be someplace better than the North Shore. People better than those people. Someone like you. But I couldn't imagine them, so I took the people I had and dressed them up to make them possible. Even real."

She had her feet up in the air and looked about fourteen. She sketched in a few real people with her hands and then dropped them. "Are you hungry? This mistress better keep her mind on her . . . lover's stomach."

I remembered that she had said she invented the magic valley because if she was Arabella Anorexia, then everyone else was a joke, too. I was going to ask her about that, but then I figured out that it was probably just another way of saying the same thing, so I only said, "I guess we could order."

After a lot of discussion, I had a double porterhouse with several side dishes, and she had a cheese omelette, all by itself. While we were waiting for the food, I took a little nap, to make up for what I had missed the night before. It was the short kind—not more than fifteen minutes—that really does a lot for you. When I woke up, she was sitting in a chair looking at me.

"You're so peaceful when you're asleep. Of course, you're always peaceful, but even more so."

"You were looking at me all the time."

"Not true. I crept around, snooped into closets. This really is an awful hotel. Then I looked out the window, down on the teeming millions, and wondered what it all meant. New York can always make you wonder that." I was very relaxed and conscious of how easy I felt with her. She made everything pleasant.

Lunch arrived, pushed in by two waiters, and it took them a long time to get the covers off and everything arranged.

"How's the steak?" Arabella asked casually after they left, playing with her omelette.

"Fair."

"It didn't look sensational when he uncovered it."

"It's passable."

"I could marry you. Could you marry me?"

She said it the way you'd ask someone to pass the salt, but I knew it was a real question. She didn't mean would we ever get married, or that she'd ever have to want to marry me, or me her. It was that she felt easy with me, and she wondered if I felt easy with her.

"Yes, I could," I said.

"You're kidding. I'm a neurotic."

"I don't care what you are—I feel comfortable with you."

"You mean all the weaknesses—the playing with everything, especially food—doesn't bother you?"

"If I'm bothered, I don't know it. I do know the other—that I'm comfortable with you."

"You seem to have all those answers down pat."

"I always know where I'm comfortable and where I'm not. I don't have to think about it."

"You really aren't kidding?"

"No. I never kid about anything like that." I don't, either.

She didn't say anything for a minute. Then she said,

154

"I'm glad, because I'm so comfortable with you . . . and because I can do something for someone else, I'm not completely useless . . . but let's not get heavy."

"Oh, I don't know, sometimes it's fun to be heavy."

"Boys never like it when a girl's heavy."

"That's right—but you're not heavy that way."

"What's the difference?"

"I don't know. I've been trying to figure it out. I think it's because you're never heavy even when you seem to be."

"Hmmmmm . . . don't know if that sounds good or not. Now let's clean this mess up."

She piled the plates and covers on the carts and wheeled them out.

"They block the hall completely," she said when she came back. " 'Remains of Olmstead Lunch Bring Hotel Traffic to Standstill.' " She came behind the chair where I was and put her arms on my shoulders. "That was the best lunch I ever had, and now you're going out, just as we said, and I'll see you at four." She kissed me on the top of the head. "I know we could call that plan off, but we won't."

"We have too much character."

"Right."

So I pulled on my topcoat and started to leave. In the hallway she said, "I'm not going to kiss you good-bye, it's too ordinary. Besides, I kiss you all the time."

I put my arms around her and kissed her. "I didn't know you wanted to be kissed," I said. "I thought you were above all that."

"There's a lot you don't know about me. No, I take that back—you have me taped."

155

"I didn't know you were a big-time rider."

"I'm really good, that's true. But I've never had my heart in horses."

"You're not alone."

"I'll bet."

As I was opening the door she said, "That was a lovely kiss."

"I thought so."

"Keep on kissing like that and you might make it."

"Is that a hint?"

"Yes, but you have to go."

Outside, the carts were blocking the hall, but the elevators were in the other direction.

When I left the Morville, I walked over to the West Side and then down to Forty-second Street. I didn't know why, but I wanted to be over there with the movie houses and lights and crowds and dirt—all the sordid mess of New York. It was so different from what I had left—not the hotel, because that was only on the surface—but Arabella and her clean rightness. I don't mean I wanted to get away from her into sordidness, but that I wanted to let everything that had happened in the past couple of days sink into me without thinking about it, and the best place to do that was in a completely different atmosphere.

So I walked along in that crowd, and there was such a collection of strange clothes and styles that my size and the bandage didn't seem that different. A few people stared, but nothing like the stares on the respectable East Side.

I didn't want to think about Arabella, but I couldn't help it. When she'd piled the dishes on the carts and gotten rid of them and then sent me off, she'd acted differently than she ever had before. She'd been efficient and disciplined. She had seemed so helpless until then, but in that moment she had seemed so independent. More so, I mean, than the ordinary girl who's partly independent all the time, but you know she couldn't do anything in a real emergency. That moment of Arabella's independent efficiency was more like the real thing. You could see her then as a girl from a long time ago, with a long dress and a bonnet on, defending a log cabin against Indians or something.

She was dreamy and romantic and cowardly and probably nuts—so different from most of the people I knew who passed for realistic—and yet she was hard in a way, too, harder than they could ever be or imagine being. And . . . her mouth was soft when I kissed her, not tense at all, and surprisingly generous. No, that wasn't surprising—after all, she had a big mouth, so why shouldn't it be generous? What was surprising was that it wasn't tense. Arabella was sensual as well as everything else.

A big black bumped into me and said, "Goddamned honky taking up the whole sidewalk, watch where you're going, you mother, you hear me?"

He was about thirty and looked fairly tough. I knew he had two friends just behind me, because I could see them out of the corner of my eye.

"Sorry," I said, "I've got leukemia and I don't see so good."

He looked uncertain and came up close to me. "Leukemia? On your head?"

"That's where I stumbled and fell last night and cut

myself open. Eight stitches. I guess my condition is getting worse."

"Yeah?" He looked as if he couldn't believe it, but kind of liked the effort put into it. "Well, be careful," he said, about half-and-half threat and helpful advice, and he and his friends went on ahead.

I could have gone up to Dad's office—it was only a couple of blocks away now, but it wasn't the day for that. And I could have gone to a movie, but I didn't feel like it. So I just walked. Down Eighth to Thirty-fourth, and then over to Penn Station and up into the Fifties on Seventh. Then back down Sixth and up Fifth. It was very cold, but as long as I kept moving it didn't bother me.

You see a lot of faces on a walk like that, and most of them pretty far down, if you're honest about it. The city itself is supposed to be collapsing financially, and the people look the same way. The whole thing is dying, like an animal hung up on barbed wire, the way I'd seen them on the ranches in Florida. It was the end of something, and there wasn't much future for whatever was coming next.

There was a collection of those monks in the orange robes in front of the library, making a lot of noise, and I looked to see if the one we'd seen changing the tire was there. I couldn't pick him out, but they all look pretty much alike. It was cold for them in those clothes, and I guess they had to jump around to keep warm.

I was going up Fifth and getting close to Central Park when I heard a woman's voice calling, "Yoo-hoo, Ox Olmstead," and turned around. She was tall and a little strange, and at first I couldn't place her. She took my hand and said, "My dear boy, always up to something dangerous. Or are you raising bees up there? You don't remember me, I can see. Mrs. Deering Gardner." Then I did remember. She was Mrs. Schrecker's sister, and I'd met her the summer I went to camp in New England and there was all the trouble about the Schreckers. Mrs. Gardner was there at the end, with Hurry-Up Hackett. She was from Boston and always seemed to wear the same dress—purple with a white collar. Or maybe she just had a lot of them.

"I cut my head," I said.

"Sorry it's not bees. They'd be so much more interesting. Did you do it yourself? Or someone else?"

"I fell on a shovel."

"That can be annoying," she said vaguely. "I'm here attending a congress on birth control. Far too many people in the world. Well, you can see that just standing here."

The crowd was jostling around us, with plenty of them staring. We were well matched.

"The question is how to get rid of people," she said. Her voice wasn't loud, but it penetrated, and some people were listening. "Shoot them? Gas them? Hitler tried all those methods and found them wanting." She had an audience by then. "So hard to cremate them all afterward, too. No, the only solution is birth control. Get them to get rid of themselves by ceasing to reproduce themselves. What do you think?"

"Sounds reasonable."

"I'm glad you think so. I always thought you were sensible. My colleagues at this congress are rather namby-pamby—they want to reduce the population for

159

economic reasons. Mine are esthetic—I see it as a way of weeding a very overgrown and unattractive garden. Good-bye, I must run. Call me in Boston."

"I'll do that, Mrs. Gardner." My feet were cold and I wanted to get going.

Just as we were moving off, a little man said to her, "Wait a minute. Was you calling people weeds?"

"I certainly was," she said calmly. "You yourself are a perfect example of the . . . "

I kept going and didn't look around. It was about four when I got back, and beginning to get dark.

The dishes were still in the corridor. I knocked at the door and got no answer. When I tried the handle it was open.

I heard the noise even before I saw her note. "They started that jackhammer just after you left. Called manager, but he said it couldn't be stopped. I've fled, back at five, when they're supposed to quit. The more you pay, the less you get, and all that stuff. *Quelle ville! Quelle pays, aussi!* Your A."

The noise was unbelievable. They were right overhead, boring through something. I called downstairs myself, and got the same story. One of those now-don't-get-excited types, what Dale Tifton would have called "your inexpensive fag," said it was very important remodeling.

"You mean that for a hundred and eight dollars I have to listen to noise like that?"

"The work is being done for customer convenience," he said.

"Not this customer."

"I'm very busy just now."

"Sorry to have bothered you," I said.

"That's quite all right," he said.

I went out and up a flight to the room where they were working. There were three of them, tearing up a bathroom floor.

"Boss says it's time to knock off," I said when I could get them to shut the thing down.

"Thought we were supposed to stay till five," one of them said, but the other two were already packing up.

"You still get paid to five," I said. "Some big shot in the hotel, Henry Kissinger, I think, is negotiating with the British, and the noise is driving them crazy."

"It'll drive them crazy all right," the one who'd wanted to stay until five said.

"They crazy already," another one said, a chunky black with a slow, powerful voice.

We all agreed that was about right.

I went back down and settled myself for a rest. Walking around that city can really tire you out.

18

I HAD DOZED OFF, and woke to find a slight breeze in my ear. Arabella was breathing into it and giggling.

"What if I were a bandit?"

"I guess I'd be taken by surprise."

"If he's not eating, he's sleeping. Never, never get ahead that way."

"I walked all over the city."

"No excuses." She danced around. "Peace has returned to the valley—to this corner of it, anyhow. How could you sleep? Wasn't that noise still going? Because it's only a few minutes after five now."

"They stopped just after I got back."

"How did you manage that?"

"They just downed tools and left."

"So you saw them leave. Ox, you did something."

"It was lucky."

"Tell me."

"Later. As you say, what a town. And country. But it can work for you sometimes, as well as against."

"It doesn't work for anyone I know. You have the touch."

"Maybe."

"All right, you're waiting for me to tell you how it went." Her voice got serious. "Ox, I could try it . . . if you were around all the time. Turning off jackhammers and giving me something to look forward to. But what does that mean? You can't be around all the time, even when you are here. And when you go back to Palm Beach—which has to be in a few months at the latest—I'd never make it. It was a very amusing idea, but it can't stand the light of day."

"I know that—it isn't your fault. As you say, no girl could be alone like that."

"I didn't say 'no girl.' I said 'very few girls.' "

"I don't count them. They'd have to be very low-geared."

"It's hard to explain, because I've been alone all my life, until I met you. I mean, I've never been frank with anyone, because I've never known anyone who wasn't weak and silly. But even so, just fighting with the weak ones is something, keeps me from going off the deep end, I know."

"I get it."

"Do you? Do you, really? Or are you covering over . . . a situation?" She looked at me hard. "I'm trying to be dead honest with you, so we don't get into a bigger mess than the one . . . I'm already in."

"I'm leveling, too."

There was a certain amount of tension in the room.

"I don't care what happens," she said. "You'll always be the most important person in the world to me. Even if I never see you again. That's not schoolgirl talk, because I'm not a schoolgirl. I know. So I want things to be straight between us more than I have ever wanted anything in my life."

I felt as though she was pushing hard, and that I was being asked for something I'd never given. I didn't know if I had it to give, or if I wanted to give it even if I could.

"You don't have to want what I want," she said, guessing what I was thinking about. "You're straight with everyone, in your way. You don't have to do any more with me than you've already done. Being straight here is my problem, not yours."

Usually when people tell you that you don't have to do anything, they don't mean it. They don't know what they're saying, for one thing. But she did, I could tell, and the same feeling came to me about her that I always got. You thought she was doing one thing—being a hopeless nut, or fool, or neurotic, or putting you in a bind—but it always turned out another way. She could be doing those things all right, but underneath there was something else, something more. She played close to the line, but she always came through. I'd always been surprised by that, but this time my heart really went out to her. I liked her and admired her in a way I had never done with anyone else.

"You're all right," I said. I had to say something, feeling that way. "At the bottom, inside you, you're all right. Never forget that."

"You really mean it?"

"Never meant anything more."

"You'd bet on me?"

"That's right."

"That's all I need," she said slowly, and went over and looked out the window.

Neither one of us said anything for a while.

She turned around and her face was wet with tears.

"That's all I need," she said. "I can go back now. I can stick it."

"Are you sure?"

"Uh-huh . . . Listen, I'm not crying because I'm sad. Just the opposite . . . but you know that."

"I know that."

She came over and sat in my lap and curled in next to me. She was very light for her height and size. And for a tall girl who was all bones, she was very soft and warm and comfortable.

We just sat like that for a long time. Her head was on my chest and her shining hair was spread all over. She was breathing so regularly I thought she was asleep. And then she woke up, and I knew she had been asleep.

We talked about what she'd do. She had to go back, and I'd try to help her. Maybe through Dad, somehow, to make it easier on her. She and I would stay in touch after I went back to Palm Beach, and try to see each other once in a while. In a couple of years she'd get out and be on her own and then . . . but we didn't talk about what would happen then.

"We should go fairly soon," she said. "Am I heavy?"

"No."

"I'll sleep with you before we go if you want," she said in a matter-of-fact way.

"What made you say that?"

"I want to cross all the t's. I don't imagine it would be very thrilling. Just another scrawny virgin. But I'm yours if you want me. Don't you think it's more dignified to say it like that than wonder? Or paw around?"

"I'll take the offer under advisement."

"You know I don't want to, don't you." She turned and put her arms against my chest so she was looking at me. "But do you know why?"

"You're saving yourself for another. For Winston Lochmann."

She waved her hand impatiently. "That was a joke. And certainly doesn't mean anything now. I told you that to keep you walking after you were hit. It worked, too."

I had an idea there was more to it than that, but I let it pass.

She couldn't, though. "Well, if I'm going to go into everything, there was something there. Andy Candy asked me a year ago if I didn't think Winston Lochmann was an 'interesting and cultured man,' and I knew what was on his mind. Then Winnie-the-Poop himself came around a few times and I gathered from the stars in his eyes that he was already counting his blessings. I thought it was funny—and trouble-making, the worst thing I could think of to do—to string him along, but I'd never have done it. I might marry for money, but it would be big money, not that chicken feed. And not a twit like that. I told you about it in a good cause—to keep you going—but I felt awful when I realized you might believe it. That's why I was sulking the rest of the way to Severn House.

"Anyhow, let's drop that, it's not important. Except . . . it shows you that I care what you think. I care for you in so many ways, Ox. . . . I'll tell you one, something girls are not supposed to do. I often go to the place we met, our special place, even on a day when I know you're not coming, just to be where you've been, where we've been. . . . How's that for being smitten right where it counts?"

She pushed an imaginary dagger into her heart and fell back. But she was up in a moment and very business-like.

"Now let's really drop that goo. Don't tease, I want to tell you something much more important, why I don't want to sleep with you even though I'm really wild about you, and perfectly willing to, even with that bandage covering half of you up. I don't want to because everyone our age does it. They all screw like rabbits, and they're all so awful that I have a horror of doing anything they do."

"It's not a bad reason."

"I hate them," she said with a lot of feeling. "It's all very well to say . . . when we were talking before . . . that they're sick. But sick or not, they take up all the air, and I hate them for it. Ever stand outside a public school and watch them file out, shambling along, dead faces, eyes on the ground, mouths hanging open, walk like their backs are broken? Or a private school, same thing. All dressed alike, girls and boys in those awful pants, sloppy clothes . . . the girls just like the boys, can't tell them apart. Like squaws, for all the talk about women's lib, shambling along behind. Walking like the boys, trying to be boys. I hate them because they frighten me. They're like some huge blob from outer space that's going to eat everyone and everything. None of them are individual, they all melt together, they're not human anymore . . . and . . ."

She was talking so fast and getting so excited that it

bothered me. But then she got a grip on herself and stopped.

"Forgive me," she said. "I get going and I shouldn't. It's part of being neurotic. But they do frighten me, and I hate them, and I don't want to be like them. And that's why I don't want to sleep with you. Otherwise . . . I'd love to. If it were a hundred years ago, and we were almost the only young people doing . . . such a thing, it would be so different—isn't that strange? I will anyhow, of course, if you want," she added anxiously. "It's just that I don't want to because of . . . what I told you, and I don't want you to be disappointed, because I'd probably be the lousiest lay . . . in the whole valley."

It was up to me to say something.

"I want to have fun with you," I said. "It's not the time—it would spoil our fun."

"You're perfect," she said, and put her head back. We stayed like that for a while before we left, looking out the window at the lights and not saying anything. It was very peaceful. Everything seemed settled, as well as it could be, and there was nothing more that had to be said. Or that could be said.

So we just sat there, and it was very quiet and pleasant and comfortable. More that way than anything that had ever happened to me. She was so right in my arms, so light and easy and close, and I felt so good holding her . . . a feeling of real happiness came over me, and it was so strong that I wondered if it was what they call love. I guess it was, I don't see how it could have been anything else. She moved just a bit herself then, as if to tell me she felt what I felt, and I tightened my arms a bit to tell her I knew. It was all very simple and easy and complete.

168

19

I GOT BACK ABOUT NINE. Dad wasn't sore, but he was curious.

"What were you doing?"

"Trying to get things settled. I called to say I'd be late."

"Hans gave me the message, but it was garbled. How'd it go?"

"She couldn't take it hiding out alone. You can't blame her. She's gone back, thinks she can stick it out for a year until she's old enough to get out."

"Probably better," Dad agreed.

"Here's the rest of the five hundred. I spent a little over a hundred."

Normally he would have asked me on what, but he didn't. Then he did the next thing that wasn't normal.

"You keep it for a while," he said. "Use it as you have to. And you don't have to account for it."

He wasn't looking at me, and I could tell he wasn't waiting for me to say thanks, so I did.

"Forget it," he said. Then he did look at me. "She is all right, isn't she?"

"Seems to be."

"I hope so. She's a nice girl."

I don't think I'd ever heard Dad call anyone nice. It wasn't his kind of word. I didn't want to talk about any of it anymore, and it didn't seem like he did, either. And Sally came along then anyhow. She didn't ask any questions, but I felt sure Dad would tell her everything.

When I went out to the kitchen to have some warmed dinner, Hans was all over me about how I should have let him drive me back.

"How was you finally coming, by train?"

"Yes."

"Then by taxi from Locust Valley?"

"Right."

"With all those cars here."

We'd come on different trains. "They're so awful," she said. "No point in spoiling all this with a dirty train ride." The dishes were still in the hall when we left. "Probably be there when the Viet Cong march in," she said.

She was right about the trains, and I was glad we weren't together. I sat in the bar car because it seemed more lively, but the commuters getting drunk were actually further down than the others. And Dad was right, there were bullet holes, lots of them.

While I was eating, Hans went out to answer the door, and when he came back he said it was Mr. Lochmann calling.

"What kind of man is he?" I asked Hans.

"He was always very nice and easy to get along with," Hans said.

"Only one problem, he has no money," Carmen said. "All in painting."

"That was it," Hans said with a sigh. "He was having no money. We were always having a struggle to get the grocery money out from him. And our wages. And he was owing money everywhere."

"How'd you happen to go to work for him in the first place?"

"We was looking for work, the usual way."

"You don't mind if I ask you sort of a personal question?"

"No, Ox, you ask anything," Carmen said.

"It never bothered him that you were Germans?"

"No, no," Hans said. "He was speaking German and loving German painting and culture, he liked us *because* we were being German. Some friends of his were saying to him that he was wrong to have Germans in his house after . . . everything that happened. But he was saying that was then, and this is now, and you should not have been holding crimes against every member of a race. He was very broad-minded that way."

Hans and Carmen were both looking at me with those simple faces of theirs, and you had to wonder if they were really that simple or if they had been Nazis. And what Mr. Lochmann really thought of them.

After I ate I drifted back to the sunken living room, where the three of them were having a drink.

Mr. Lochmann jumped up and said it was awful that I'd been hit, but he spoiled the effect when he giggled and added that he didn't really understand what it was all about.

He sat down and they started talking about this and that again. I watched Mr. Lochmann and could see that he was even more nervous than usual.

"Hope you like it here," he kept saying to Dad, and

Dad kept answering, "Like it fine," and waiting for him to get to the point.

But he couldn't. His head was bobbing up and down, and the dandruff was falling, but he couldn't say what was on his mind. He looked so pathetic you couldn't believe that there were corpses behind him, the way Sally had said there always were behind gigglers. And yet, there was something a little sinister about him.

He finally got around to me again. "Carmen says she enjoys cooking for you," he said. He told me he called the house every so often to talk to her and Hans in German. He was living in the city with his mother and I guess it was lonely.

"She's a good cook," I said. "And she and Hans say they like working for you a lot."

"Oh, they're all right," he said. "Hans is a rotten butler," he said with a giggle, "and Carmen much too heavy a cook for my taste, but they mean well, and we're all used to each other."

"Weren't you worried when you hired them?" I asked him.

"What about?"

"Oh, you know, all that talk about Germans coming from South America being Nazis."

"Oh, I'm sure they were Nazis," he said. "My idea was that that would make them work all the harder for an American. They'd be afraid not to, with all that guilt. And it worked, up to a point. I mean, up to the point of their irreducible laziness."

He sort of fooled me with that. It was a hard way to look at things, not as soft as the rest of what he did and said.

He wasn't hard in his talk with Dad and Sally in the

next fifteen minutes before he left, though. He was very nervous, and seemed miserable about it, too.

After he'd gone, Sally told me everything had been quiet all day. "If you discount Mr. Lochmann's visit."

"He was sent to terminate the lease, I'm sure," Dad said. "But he lost his nerve. What was that you were asking him about Hans and Carmen?"

"Ted says they have to be Nazis, coming up from South America after the war."

Dad grunted. "Ordinarily you're not curious about those political details. What do you make of Lochmann?" he asked Sally.

"Tonight? I agree—the lease. Generally? He'd bite you if he could."

"He's an odd one," Dad said.

"He's a mystifier," Sally said.

"What's that?" Dad asked her.

"People who feel inadequate try to mystify other people to make themselves important. He hired Hans and Carmen so people would wonder why he did it. Everything is designed to create interest. It's basically cheap, a cheap trick by a cheap person."

"Some insight you've got."

"I can't stand people like that," she said. "But there are more important things to worry about. Ox, I hate to think of Arabella back there at Myrtle Grove."

"So do I. But she seems to have gotten her feet under her. She may be able to handle it."

"If she can't, I'll take her someplace myself," Sally said. "I would have done it today if you and Barry hadn't taken everything into your own hands. Naturally she wasn't going to go off on her own. How the two of you could have dreamed that up is beyond me."

"It didn't seem like such a bad idea at the time," I said, sticking up for Dad a little, the first time I'd ever done that.

"Men's ideas never do, to men," she said.

"My God, women's lib," Dad said, but he wasn't really sore.

"Not me," Sally said. "That's the way our grandmothers talked, and they were right."

"How's all this going to work?" Dad asked me. "Will she let you know what's happening?"

"She'll call tomorrow," I said.

"Poor kid," Sally said.

"She's nice, but she's a neurotic," Dad said. "You told me yourself that anorexia was a neurotic disease," he said to Sally with just a touch of apology. He'd come down somewhat in his high opinion of Arabella. A couple of hours before, she'd been only nice. Now she was neurotic, too. I figured that was because he and Sally had talked about her before Mr. Lochmann had come. They both liked her, but when two people talk they always end up with a lower opinion than what either of them have alone.

They were waiting for me to say something, so I did. "She *is* neurotic," I said. "She may make it and she may not. I guess everyone has to do that on their own."

They were relieved. They'd been worried that I was so fond of her that I could have overlooked the fact she was neurotic.

"At the same time, though, I feel I ought to help her if I can," I went on. "It's like one of your wild animals," I said to Dad. "When they're hurt or sick is when they deserve more help, not less. So I'll help her if I can."

174

They nodded to that. "And I won't stand by and watch anyone be cruel to her." That was a little tougher to take, but they accepted it. I could see by their expressions that I'd checked out—realistic, but kind.

"I think we all feel that way," Dad said. "I proved it by taking a sock at Big Andy on her behalf, and telling off Revere."

"I guess you did," I said. He hadn't done those things for Arabella, but if he wanted to say so it was all right with me. It was something he could be reminded of later if necessary.

"You put it well, Ox," Sally said. "I'll back you up."

She was more human than Dad and understood more of what Arabella was and what she meant. Not in the personal sense, to me or anyone else, but because there was only one of her and she was worth a lot. Particularly in these times.

"Now that that's all settled, at least for the moment, what about Christmas?" Sally asked us.

"Christmas?" Dad looked at her blankly.

"Yes, Christmas. It's in four days. What are you planning?"

Dad and I looked at each other. "Nothing," Dad told her. "We never do anything about Christmas."

"You mean no tree. But you . . ."

"I mean nothing," Dad said. "No tree, no presents, no big meal, nothing. In the first place, everyone in my . . . so-called family gets enough stuff during the year. In the second place, I think it's all a lot of commercial crap."

"I can take it or leave it myself," Sally said. "But it seems different up here when it's cold than in Palm

Beach. And Hans and Carmen are pressing me to do something."

"Tell them to do it in their own quarters," Dad said.

Sally was looking at me and I shrugged. "Christmas doesn't mean anything to me," I said. It didn't, either.

Sally left us soon after that, and I asked Dad if he'd pressed charges against Big Andy.

"I have ten days to do it," he said. "I've been stalling to see what happens. Funny they didn't howl today to get Arabella back."

"Maybe they don't want her back."

"Maybe," Dad said. "But I'm sure they're dog-in-the-manger about her. They want her if someone else has her, or if she goes off on her own. And then once they have her, they don't want her."

"Sounds right. How's FRAAN going?"

"Not bad. We have auditors coming out our ears, and they don't see the end yet. They've found a lot of the money—Bones put it in the wrong bank. He'd opened an account with Chemical, also in FRAAN's name, although the organization banked regularly with Chase. He thought it was a good idea to spread it around. Then he forgot all about it. Now they figure there must be one more bank involved and he's trying to remember. How's your head?"

"Not bad. Stitches come out next week."

"That's good."

Our new-style conversations weren't much, but they were something compared to the way we used to talk.

When I went to bed I lay awake a long time, worrying about Arabella, imagining the worst she could have run into.

20

SHE WAS SUPPOSED TO CALL BY TEN, and I was up in plenty of time. I waited until eleven before I told Dad. He'd stayed to see what was happening.

"That's too bad," he said, "but there's nothing we can do. If you don't hear from her by tomorrow morning, I'll file against Andy. Otherwise, there's nothing we can do. She's Andy's kid, and that's that. . . . Do you hear me, Ox?"

"Yes, I hear you."

"Do you understand?"

"Yes, I understand." I knew he was right, technically.

"Ox, don't get any fancy ideas—don't you go over there."

I thought he was going to ask me to promise him not to go, and I was ready to give him all the promises he wanted. I guess he felt that, because he didn't ask for any.

He left for the city then, and five minutes later I was on my way out, too, when Sally called to me. "Wait a minute, I'll go with you."

"Maybe you wouldn't want . . ."

"I know where you're going," she said, "and two is better than one."

"Dad told me not to go. If you go with me, he'll be sore at you."

"I'm going to help you. He won't be sore about that."

"I'm going to push this," I warned her. "Dad doesn't want to push it. I don't blame him, but that could mean trouble between me and him. You'd have to be on his side in the end, so maybe you'd better not get on my side in the beginning. If I go alone, I know where I stand. If you go with me, I don't, because I don't know how long you'll be able to stick it."

"I'll stick it this morning, all the way." Her face was set and she looked like a different woman from the one in Palm Beach a few months before. "My trouble's never been lack of courage, Ox—I've been through some terrific fights and never backed down—but boredom. And I'm not bored now. You can count on me completely this morning. After that, we'll . . . go over the position, and I'll go on or get out. How's that?"

It was straight and I told her so.

"One detail," she said. "Have you thought of calling her first?"

"Yes, but I have to figure that if she didn't call, someone stopped her and I'm not going to be able to get through to her, so it will just tip them off."

"Probably right. Let's take the big car, and Hans. The more the better in this sort of thing. Give me five minutes to change."

I was afraid Hans would be so curious that we'd have to think about him too much, but for once he was quiet and calm. "He *is* a kraut," Sally said to me as we rolled out, "and they do enjoy a fight."

"So do you." She was very calm herself.

"I have nothing to lose," she said. "It's easy to be calm when you have nothing to lose." She had on a fur coat and looked very well.

It was bitter cold that day, even colder than the day before. And not sunny anymore, but cloudy and windy.

We swept in the main drive of Myrtle Grove, and followed it for half a mile until the main house loomed up. There were knots of gardeners working along the way, getting the leaves up and putting burlap over the boxwoods and jobs like that. They scarcely looked up— so many limousines came in there that an ordinary car would have attracted more attention.

"You know where Mr. Marlborough's house is, Hans?" Sally asked him on the intercom.

"Yes, I was having been there."

We wound past other houses and outbuildings and garages and gardens and tennis courts and other stuff. Then we came around a sharp corner and there it was, a simple but pretty attractive colonial house, gray with white shutters and trim. On the lawn was a neat sign that said Andrew F. Marlborough.

Sally sort of winced at the sign. "He is far down, isn't he."

"Lizzie made him put it there—even he knows better than that."

Hans pulled into the driveway and we got out and walked up to the door. Hans waited in the car.

When we got there, Sally and I looked at each other to see who would press the buzzer. She pointed her gloved finger at me. "You have the honor," she said.

I pressed and we waited. Fifteen, twenty seconds. I pressed again. I had the feeling that the place was empty, or almost empty. I mean, I didn't feel there were twenty people on the other side of the door holding their breath.

It finally opened on the third ring, and there was a woman in her forties, sort of faded.

"Yes?"

"Is Arabella here?" I asked her.

"Are you friends of hers?"

"Yes."

"She's not here just now."

"Are you her mother?" Sally asked.

"Yes, I am," Mrs. Marlborough said. She put her hand up to her hair and pushed it around. "I'm her mother."

She was very vague and her clothes were the same way. Not exactly messy, but with no life to them, either. She looked even less like Arabella than Big Andy did. You couldn't even say she might have been pretty once—she looked like she'd always been the way she was.

"She came back last night," Sally prompted her.

"My, yes, and rather late." She looked at me. "You must be the one who's caused all the trouble. . . . I'd ask you in," she said to Sally, "but I haven't . . . why don't you come in anyhow?"

She backed out of the doorway and we followed her. I expected a kind of shabbiness, but everything was very neat and pulled together. And expensive, with a lot of early American antiques.

Sally kept after her. "Then this morning she got up and went somewhere?"

"She went with Big Andy," Mrs. Marlborough said.

She said his name as though there was nothing strange about having a husband called Big Andy, which made it seem all the stranger.

"Alone?"

Mrs. Marlborough stared at her, and Sally tried again.

"Just Arabella and . . . Big Andy? No one else?"

"Oh, no. Just the two of them."

"What time was that?"

"About half past eight." She was like an obedient child and would have answered questions all day, I guess.

"Do you have any idea of where they went?"

"I think to the main house. To Mrs. Revere's house."

There was nothing more she could tell us. I was sure Arabella was not in the house. Sally was, too, I could tell. So we started to leave.

"Wouldn't you like to stay and have some coffee. Or a drink?" As Sally said later, "Poor thing, she was told once that some people like a snort early in the morning." I myself was thinking then that Arabella was right, she was pretty far gone.

"No, we have to run," Sally said.

"Any message for Arabella?" She was looking at us without any deception, and it seemed to me she really did think Arabella would be back.

"Ask her to call," Sally said.

"I will," Mrs. Marlborough promised.

We got back in the car and told Hans to go on to the main house.

"Wow," Sally said. "That one's really tranquilized. Valium coming out the ears. When that Big Andy gets through with them they're really gone for good."

I was thinking that the house was sadder for being

neat than if it had been a mess. I could see why that small neat house had worked on Arabella, because it was so different from her parents, who weren't a bit neat inside, but all torn up.

"You handled it perfectly," I told Sally. "And don't say, 'Flattery will get you nowhere.'"

"She never asked my name," Sally said, shaking her head. "I was on the verge of giving it to her once, but decided she'd only forget it. She knew you, though—if only as 'the troublemaker'—so I guess Arabella will get the message when she . . . comes back."

"I don't think she's coming back here," I said. "They kept her from calling, which means they have plans, and I don't think those plans include her coming back."

"Neither do I," Sally said. "I knew that as soon as I said it."

We were at the main house by then.

"Shall I keep on talking?" Sally asked me. "Until the dice get cold?"

"Fine with me."

A butler answered the door almost as soon as I rang. He wasn't the same one Arabella and I had seen setting the table.

"We're looking for Andrew Marlborough," Sally said. "His wife told us he came up this way this morning."

"He has an office in the west wing," the butler said with some doubt in his voice. "You could try there. It's just around the . . . "

"There must be an inside entrance," Sally said smoothly, stepping into the hall. "We'll go that way."

"But, madam . . . " the butler began, looking at her and then taking in the size of the car outside and not sure which way to go.

"If you'll show us the way," Sally said firmly, and he gave in.

We walked behind him for a long time, down one enormous corridor after another. None of them looked like what I'd seen with Arabella. They were more like rooms than corridors, twenty feet wide, the walls covered with paintings and tapestries. Off those long corridor-rooms, other rooms opened, huge, filled with antique furniture and more art.

"It's a museum," Sally whispered. "This stuff must be worth millions. Tens of millions."

The butler walked ahead of us with a lot of disapproval in his back.

The corridors started tapering down—we were getting into less expensive territory.

The butler stopped in front of a door and knocked. He knocked again and there was still no answer.

"Mr. Marlborough is evidently not there," he said, enjoying that.

"Then where shall we find him?"

"I'm sure I don't know. I doubt if he is on the grounds."

Sally opened the door before he could stop her and looked in. Then she shook her head and said, "Negative." I could see a corner of the office—as neat as his house and just as depressing.

"Where does he park his car?" I asked.

"He doesn't always leave it in the same place," the butler answered.

"Is Mrs. Revere here?" Sally asked him.

"I don't know . . . but even if she is, she can't be disturbed."

"It's very important."

"I'm sorry. I will show you back to the front door."

Sally looked at me helplessly. She could tell he wasn't going to let her snow him again.

"You'll take us to Mrs. Revere," I said.

"I shall do no such thing." His old eyes had fire in them all of a sudden, even if his chin was trembling. "If you don't leave immediately, I'll call the . . ."

I did the only thing I could do. Or anyone can do, if they want to make their point and still keep from fighting. Picked him up by the front, a handful of shirt and vest and coat. When his feet got clear of the ground he tried to kick me.

"You'll take us," I said.

"I will not," he choked, still kicking.

"You'll take us or I'll peel off all your clothes and turn you loose on the lawn."

It got to him. He was so wild that a threat to hurt him wouldn't have meant a thing. But the idea of that old naked body being seen and laughed at by everyone on the place cooled him off.

"All right," he gasped out, and I put him back on the floor. "I'll take you, but I warn you that you're going to be arrested for this. You won't get off the place without being caught."

"That's up to Mrs. Revere, isn't it?" Sally asked him.

"I know what she'll say," he said with satisfaction.

So we worked our way back through the corridors and then up a tremendous staircase and through another maze of big corridors on the second floor. The bedroom doors were closed up there.

The butler knocked at a set of double doors, and a woman opened one of them.

"To see Mrs. Revere," the butler said, every inch the perfect servant again.

The woman stared at him. "She can't be disturbed. You know that, Dorkins. She's doing the accounts . . . "

"I was given no choice, Mrs. Potter. They forced their way in."

"Forced their way in? Why didn't you call the police?"

"They overpowered me."

"Then I'll do it myself." She turned from the door.

"I wouldn't be in such a hurry," Sally said, and Mrs. Potter stopped, thrown off by the insider's voice and manner. "Just tell Mrs. Revere we're here. Better yet, we'll tell her ourselves."

"You wait right . . . " Mrs. Potter began, but Sally was already going past her, and I was right behind, with one hand bringing Dorkins along, too.

Inside, a short corridor led to another door, and we went through that into a sitting room. At the far end was a doorway to a bedroom. The sitting room was large but not too much so, and not furnished the way the rooms downstairs were. More in a normal way, with just a few old things around. At one end was a desk, and there was Lizzie, pen in hand, her head turning toward us.

She was surprised, but only for an instant. Then the back hunched a little more and the head shot out. "How did these people get in here?"

"We're looking for Andrew Marlborough and his daughter," Sally said sweetly. "If you'll tell us where they are, we'll leave quietly. There's no need to get excited, we're not burglars."

"You're trespassers," Lizzie said. "I recognize you,"

she said to me. "The . . . destructive boy. I'm happy to see that some destruction . . . came your way."

"Tell us where Arabella is," I said.

"I don't know where she is," she said crossly. "Dorkins, call the police."

"I can't, madam. He's holding me."

"You call," she said to Mrs. Potter.

"Nobody's going to call," I said. "And until you tell us where Arabella is, nobody's going to leave this room."

There was a telephone on the desk and Lizzie made a grab for it. I kept one hand on Dorkins and pulled the phone away from her with the other. "I mean it," I told her.

I guess something about my attitude and what had happened a couple of days before cooled her off.

"I told you I don't know where she is," she said. "I don't keep track of the comings and goings of everyone who lives here. Especially of someone like . . . that girl."

"Her father has taken her somewhere," I said. "He'd never have done it without checking with you, because it's all tied into a lot of other things . . . the trouble I had here, all the rest. You know. Now tell us."

No one said anything.

Finally Lizzie said, "The girl's unbalanced. She's a . . ."

"Where is she?" I was about ready to throw Dorkins at her and I guess she knew it.

"She's been taken to an . . . institution."

"What institution?"

"I don't know . . . "

"What institution?"

"Kensington."

"Where is it?"

"In Connecticut—near New Haven." She didn't seem upset anymore, but acted like she had the situation well under control. "I don't think you'll be going there, though," she said. "And even if you did, it wouldn't do you any good. Presumptuous people like you can't . . . "

"Let's go," I said to Sally.

Lizzie sort of wanted us to stay by then, until she'd finished telling us off, and when she saw we were leaving she leaned forward and hissed, "I hope the police *kill* you!"

"Watch that dribble on your chin," Sally said. "Takes away from your natural beauty."

We left fast. Back to the stairs and down to the front hall and out the door.

"Move it," I told Hans as we piled in, and he wheeled the car away and down the main driveway.

We only had about a quarter mile to go when we saw the police cars drawn up across the road, and the cops standing there with riot guns.

Hans slowed down and gave himself a quick cross. "I was not able to get by them," he said.

"Can you turn around?"

"No, and besides there was one behind us."

I looked and there was. We were stopped by then.

"Was I should be full steam and bust through maybe and probably not?" Hans asked calmly.

"No," I said. "We're in enough trouble as it is."

"She must have had an alarm button somewhere," Sally said.

"What shall we have been doing?" Hans asked, still calm.

"Doesn't make much difference," I told him. "They're going to arrest me for sure. Sally maybe, and you maybe not. Tell 'em you only drove. Call Dad as soon as you can. Tell him what happened to us and that Arabella's in a place called Kensington. I can't think of anything else. Can you?" I asked Sally.

"Negative," she said. "That covers it."

The cops were around the car by then, about ten of them with their guns, and Hans rolled the window down.

"Hello, Hans . . . We have a complaint against . . . the people in the rear," one of them said, speaking very slowly and stumbling over his words. "Trespassing, breaking and entering, assault and battery." He was confused and embarrassed.

"What you were wanting us to do, then?" Hans asked him. "Follow you to the station?"

"No, this is too serious for that . . . technique. The . . . people in the rear will have to come with us. You only sat in the car, didn't you? I mean, you only drove them?"

"I was not moving out," Hans said.

"Then you can go," the cop said, sort of relieved.

He came to the back door, but we were already getting out.

Sally held her arms out with her wrists together. "Go ahead," she said, "put them on me."

"Aren't you . . . the lady who's rented at Severn House?"

"That's right—and I need not add that when Mr. Olmstead finds out about this, there'll be a dynamite reaction."

"I can't help that," he said. "These are serious charges. I am sorry, though. No, we're not going to handcuff you. As long as you come peacefully."

So we climbed into the back of a patrol car and were driven off. Hans waved and we waved back.

21

WE WERE BOOKED into the jail at Mineola. That's in the middle of Long Island, about ten miles from Locust Valley. They said later I should have been put somewhere else, because I was a juvenile, but my size and the cops being so excited were hard on the rule book, and the details got overlooked.

I was put in a cell by myself, and Sally and I winked at each other as I went off. It had been a full morning, and I lay down for a nap before lunch. The cells on both sides were empty, and there were no distractions from the ones that were occupied farther along.

When lunch came it was terrible.

"I can't live on stuff like this," I told the guard.

"You'll have to. I can bring you more."

"Quantity wouldn't help. It's just no good." It was all white bread and soggy vegetables, with a little piece of dried-out meat of some kind floating like a towel on a wet bathroom floor. But I knew I had to eat or I'd go under. "Wait a minute," I called after him as he was moving off. "I will take seconds on it."

"You haven't started on what's there."

"No, but I know myself."

So he brought me another plate and slopped the same mess on it and I ate both of them. It was hard going, but I got them down.

After that there was nothing to do except lie on your bunk, and mine was about two feet too short for me, so it wasn't very comfortable.

The only thing you could do was think, and there was nothing I wanted to think about. Everything looked bad in all directions.

So I just lay there and let the minutes and the hours go by. The only surprise was that it was so hot. I had thought jails were supposed to be cold, but this one was steaming.

At about four, Dad came down the corridor with Bones Blossom and some other man I'd never seen.

"You need a bigger bunk," Dad said.

"I know it."

"Sally's out on bail, and you should be, too, but those damned Waterlukkers have brought pressure to bear, and the judge won't set bail for you until tomorrow. There'll be a hearing then, and bail will be set and you'll get out. For now it looks like a night in the pokey. Won't kill you."

"Do you want anything to read?" Bones asked me.

"He's not long on reading," Dad said.

"I'm glad Sally's out," I said to Dad.

"I called Kensington about Arabella. Can't get information on the phone. Sally and I will take the chopper up tonight . . . oh, this is my lawyer, Sam Farnsworth. He's with O'Neill and Butler, in the city, the people who handle all my work up here."

"Glad to meet you, Ox," Mr. Farnsworth said.

"Bones is a lawyer, too," Dad said. "A lot of talent here."

"I used to be a pretty good one," Bones said. "Better than I am at accounting."

"You were very good," Mr. Farnsworth said.

Bones wasn't listening. "Listen, Barry," he said to Dad, "that bandage . . . "

"I told you—he was slugged by the gardener, the one we've . . . "

"We might get some judge out here to issue a habeas corpus writ because of illness—what do you think, Sam?"

Mr. Farnsworth thought that over. It seemed to come as a surprise to him.

"It would take all night," I said. "I'm OK here."

"All right," Bones said. "Maybe better—might give us something to throw at them later. Like the juvenile question. Right, Sam?"

Mr. Farnsworth thought that over, too.

"You are OK, Ox?" Dad asked me.

"I'm fine." He hadn't chewed me out about disobeying him, so I said, "Sorry about going, but I had to."

"Forget it. We'll do everything we can about Arabella tonight," he promised me. "And Sam has filed assault charges against Big Andy and the gardener who hit you. And I'm pushing in the city on the Waterlukkers."

"It's not easy," Bones said, "but they do have enemies." He was as soft as ever, but he seemed efficient.

"I've got Frank Parsons on the PR," Dad said. "I

figure publicity has to be good for us and bad for them. Boy slugged, girl abducted . . . "

"I think he's right, Sam," Bones said, and I finally got it that he was kidding Mr. Farnsworth.

They told me some more and then they took off. The last thing Dad said was, "I'm in it all the way, Ox, remember that."

They were going down the corridor and then Bones came back. "Don't worry about Sam Farnsworth," he said. "Slow and conservative, but dependable. He's just never seen anything like this." He paused and then he said, "Your father has, though, and so have I. Barry's a good man in a fight, you know. So am I, even though I don't look it."

Under the softness I could sense that he wasn't talking hot air. "I believe you," I said. "Thanks for coming."

"Really a pleasure," he said, and then he went along after them.

Dinner was as bad as lunch—potatoes and turnips and a terrible salad and hot dogs and more lousy bread. I almost threw up, but I got two of them down again. I couldn't understand how I'd forgotten to ask Dad and Bones to arrange some better food.

Dad had left a card for me from Mom that said, "Finally in Buenos Aires and it's awful. How did it get such a reputation? You're better off than I am after all." It seemed to go with the place, and I borrowed some Scotch tape from the guard and put it on the wall at the back.

About eight a couple of guards brought another prisoner down the corridor and locked him into the cell next to mine. He was about fifty, medium-sized and very skinny, and looked poor but neat.

He walked around for a while and then sat on his bunk, and finally said, "I hope you're not sore at me." He had a sort of Brooklyn accent.

"Why should I be sore at you? I don't even know you."

"I'm Jack Taffle—the guy who hit you with the shovel."

I sat up. "Of course I'm sore at you, you . . . why wouldn't I be sore at you?"

"You wouldn't be sore if you understood. I had no choice. You was in the wrong." He had a long pale face and pale eyes, and a very gentle voice. I didn't know whether he was crazy or not, but he acted as though he believed what he was saying.

"You're nuts," I told him.

"Wait a minute," he said. "Do me the favor—hear me out. You was on Mrs. Revere's property. You was trespassing. She had told Eddie and Fritz to get you off and you laid hands on Eddie. How was I to know what was next? You might have assaulted Mrs. Revere. I had to defend the property—and Eddie, and her—so what could I do? I had to go on the attack."

"You could see I wasn't hurting Eddie. And that I wasn't anywhere near Lizzie. And that I was leaving."

"In a split second a guy can't see all that and make those decisions. All I knew was what I saw: Eddie up in the air, held there by this huge guy, and Mrs. Revere out of her mind. How did I know what was going to happen next?"

"You could have used your common sense."

194

"I thought I did. Now if I was wrong, that's something else, and I'll have to pay the penalty."

"You seem very calm about that."

"It's the American way," he said. "You make a mistake and you pay the penalty. It's the other side of: You do the right thing and you get the reward. That's why we're a great country. If you're right you win, and if you're wrong you lose. If you'd been a desperate character, a real criminal, like I thought you was, then I'd be a hero for slugging you. Now I'm a bum, because you're respectable. Although you're slipping, because you made a mistake going into the house today and throwing Dorkins around. Now you'll have to pay."

He had a rough accent, but he was sort of logical, and he was getting me confused.

"How do you stand working for Lizzie?" I asked him, to change the subject.

"You mean Mrs. Revere?"

"You call her Mrs. Revere. I call her Lizzie."

"Why don't you call her Mrs. Revere, too?"

"Because Lizzie sounds better. More disrespectful."

"Why do you want to be disrespectful about her?"

He never got sore about anything, just kept coming. I was trying to get him sore and I wasn't making it.

"Because she doesn't deserve any respect," I said, playing my best card. "Because she's a repulsive, nasty, selfish, mean, disgusting old woman who does terrible things to people."

"She may be all those things," Jack said without blinking, "and do all those things. But she's still a winner, and it's the winner you have to respect in this country."

"How is she a winner?"

195

"She's rich."

"So am I—what does that mean?"

"Then you're a winner, too, and I and everyone else should take their hats off to you. The whole idea of this country is to get ahead, to make money, that's what a winner is."

"What about the people who don't have any money?"

"They're losers. It's hard to respect them."

"You realize you're including yourself there?"

"Sure. I have no respect for myself. I had a lot of chances to make money. But I blew them all. I don't deserve any respect."

I was beginning to wonder if he was kidding me. But he didn't give any hint of it. His long face and pale eyes weren't excited in any way, and he acted like he believed everything he said.

"How can you live with yourself if you don't respect yourself?"

"Because I don't know if my being a loser is permanent. That's the real beauty of this country. You can be down for forty-five years, the way I've been. Then you can strike it rich and you're a winner. So as long as the *possibility* of future respect is there—and it always is—you can live without present respect."

"Don't you know that only about one person in a million ever strikes it rich? That all the rest will live and die in the jobs they have? That all those people have to live with no respect or self-respect, according to you? Isn't that an awful lot?"

"It doesn't matter. That's the way it is."

"I can even see how you might respect someone who made their own money," I told him. "But people like

Lizzie—and me—we're living off inherited money. We never did anything to get it. How can you respect that?"

"As long as you've got it, it doesn't make any difference where it came from. You're still a winner. Although you yourself aren't quite as big a winner as Mrs. Revere."

He smiled when he said that—it was the first time he'd showed any humor about anything, although he wasn't a bit gloomy in his manner. Just the opposite. He wasn't one of those soreheads who take out their bitterness in some crazy theory. If Jack was crazy, he was having fun doing it.

"Is that why you're on her side instead of mine?" I asked him. "Just because her pile is bigger than mine? Than my Dad's, I should say."

"I guess so. The bigger the winner, the bigger the respect."

"You mean that if she had me tied up and told you to shoot me, you'd do it because she was a 'bigger winner'?"

"Now hold on. I wouldn't do anything illegal for anyone, even for her."

"What about hitting me with the shovel?"

"That didn't seem illegal to me at the time—I thought the action suited the crime, looking at it from my standpoint. I can see now that I was wrong, and I'll pay the penalty. But I'd have to do the same thing all over again."

"You're all mixed up. What if you *hadn't* hit me with that shovel? What if you had just watched from the trees to see if I did anything really tough to anyone before you got into it?"

"Well, for one thing, if I'd waited I might not have had a crack at you. But the most important reason is that if I'd waited I wouldn't have been doing my duty to Mrs. Revere."

"I don't follow that. She doesn't pay you to act as a bodyguard."

"She pays me to do my job at Myrtle Grove. And part of my job is to see that what she wants gets done. She wanted you stopped, so it was my job to stop you."

"But if you hadn't, if you'd hidden in the trees, she never would have known the difference . . . no, don't tell me, *you* would have known."

"That's it, you're beginning to get it."

"What if you'd killed me?"

"Then I'd have had to pay the full penalty."

"You wouldn't have felt bad snuffing out a teenager?"

"I would have felt terrible—and you're all right, too, which makes it worse, knowing you now—but I would have felt worse if I hadn't done my duty."

I couldn't break him down. "But doesn't it bother you that it doesn't work the other way? I'll bet she doesn't feel any obligations toward you."

"Of course not. Why should she?"

That really floored me. "You mean you know that to Lizzie you're no better than a slave, and yet you have this sense of duty to her?"

"Look, if I had her money, I'd act the same way she does. I'd be just as mean and repulsive and nasty—I know she's all those things—but that's the way you are when you have money. If I was rich, I'd be just as hard on the help as she is. So how can I blame her when I'd be the same way if I was in her shoes?"

"There are people with money who aren't as bad as she is."

"Are there?" For a moment he seemed normal and cynical. "No, I'm only kidding— I know there are. Let me go back a little, because I didn't say what I meant just right there. If you have money, you have the option. That's it, you have the option. You can go good, or you can go dead mean, or anywhere in between. Now I probably wouldn't be so mean if I had her money, because . . . well, a lot of reasons. But I'd have the right to if I wanted to, and so does she. So if she decid d to go mean—and she did—I can't argue with it, any more than I could if she'd gone good."

"And what rights do you and the rest of the one hundred and ninety-nine million Americans without money have?"

"None."

"You can't be serious."

"Sure I am. We have none, because we don't have any money."

I realized there wasn't much I could say to that, because I *knew* poor people didn't have any rights, even when they thought they did. He was saying it from a different angle, but he was saying the same thing.

"If you have money, you can do anything," he went on. "And if you don't, you can't do a thing. That's what this country stands for. And if you have it, you *should* do anything you want. And if you don't have it, you shouldn't do anything."

"Just take orders from the rich?"

"That's right."

Well, I thought to myself, that's what everyone has to

do anyhow, so maybe you're smart to put a good face on it. But I had to keep arguing with him.

"You're wild," I said. "You're talking about the way things were about a thousand years ago in Europe. What they came over here to get away from."

"No, it's different. In those times, there was no chance for a man to get ahead. Just like a black couldn't get ahead in the old South. But in America you can get ahead. All the people who are at the top now came over here the same way, with nothing. Everyone had the same start. So no one has anyone to blame but himself if he didn't make it. It's not the same as the old country at all."

He was really out of this world, but it all hung together for him. It had what they call logic to it. Too much for me, I couldn't crack it. He wasn't really a fool, because he didn't deny anything—like what Lizzie was—or overlook anything. He just took the usual mess and stood it on its head. And he wasn't eating his heart out, the way most poor people do. He had his self-disrespect, or whatever you'd call it, and the rest of his picture, and he was right at home with it. Nothing bothered him. And I suspected that he knew even more than he said. He had a way of giving the whole show away so innocently, like saying the poor have no rights anyhow and have to take orders from the rich.

He was a long way from boring, and we talked a lot that night. Besides, it kept my mind off other things.

Jack lived alone in some little town on the North Shore. He had his own little house, and did everything for himself. He'd been working for Lizzie for sixteen years. She wasn't Mrs. Revere when he started—she was

Mrs. Pedley then, married to the doctor who'd gotten the ax over the curtains. Only Jack said it wasn't curtains.

"It was ladders. They were painting the north side of the main house, and she didn't like the ladders and scaffolding crisscrossing the windows. She said she felt like she was in jail when she looked outside." We were looking at each other through our bars and we grinned at the same time. "Dr. Pedley made his big mistake and laughed at that. He was gone inside a month."

"He didn't get the picture," I said.

"He lasted seven years, though."

"How long has Mr. Revere lasted?"

"He's been in there about ten. Pretty good."

"Think he might go the distance?"

"He might."

"No mistakes yet?"

"I guess not. He takes chances, though. He talks to her a lot franker than any of the others. And she lets him get away with it. I guess she's getting old."

"I'd hate to have run into her in her prime."

"I think his strong card is that even when he says something critical he doesn't laugh. The laughter—that's what she can't stand."

"Yes, that's the hardest."

"He did come close one time, though." Jack threw back his head and chuckled. He was really in a good mood by then. "It was about me sweeping up Mrs. Revere's walk. That was a favorite path of hers in the woods. She used to like to walk there—well, she still does—and she has very sensitive feet. And her walking shoes have soft soles. Anyhow, she complained to Dave

Walters—he was the superintendant then, nice guy, got fired for bad petunias—about all the sticks and stuff hurting her feet on the path. He took me down there, expecting to find some real branches, even logs.

"His face was something when he saw there were only some twigs and leaves. 'My God, Jack, these little twigs—how the hell can she feel these through her shoes?' I told him that wasn't the point—if she said she could feel them, she could. He said it was too much for him—how was he supposed to get rid of twigs? The place was already being raked twice a week, you see. This was stuff so small it would go between the rake teeth. I said I'd sweep it.

" 'You mean sweep it with a broom?' Dave asked me. I said sure. 'But it's a quarter mile, it'll take you a couple of hours.' 'If I'm not doing that, I'll be doing something else, Dave,' I told him. 'But this is all wrong,' he said. 'Sweeping twigs for that old . . . ' and he called her a name I won't repeat. 'It's like being a slave. Don't you care about that?' I told him I didn't, and he said, 'All right, if you want to do it, do it. If it was left to me, though, I'd tell her I wouldn't, and that I wouldn't order any man on the place to.'

"So I went ahead and swept it every week, and she walked out there every so often. No more complaints, everything was fine. She even said so. Until Mr. Revere came on me one day when I was sweeping away and asked me what I was doing, and I told him the leaves and twigs hurt Mrs. Revere's feet. Well, he didn't say anything, but his face told it all. He went off and we heard what happened from one of the maids. He told Mrs. Revere it was impossible that what was on that path could bother her. She listened to that for a few minutes, and then she let him have it but good. She said he had no sympathy, no understanding, what had she married—a gentleman or a tyrant? She played him like a violin, and at the end of it he was down on his knees begging her forgiveness and crying . . . "

Jack told me about the rest of the Waterlukkers, too. The four brothers and how they ran half the stuff in New York. And in Washington, too. How they were into everything you could think of, and never forgot an enemy, and what they'd do to people.

"But she's the worst," he said with pride. "The general public doesn't know about her, the way they do about her brothers, but she's the worst."

"According to the way you look at things, I guess that means you've really made it," I said. "Working for the worst, I mean."

"Oh, I'm nowhere," he said. "But if I ever did hit it, I'd sure know how to behave. I've had lessons from masters."

"What do they want?" I asked him. "I don't mean her, she's just plain vicious, but them, the brothers. They've got all the money they need. Why do they work so hard?"

"They want to keep it," he said. "They go into good works and politics and all that because they want this country to keep going, so they can hold onto what they have. That's why this country is safer than anywhere. We've got a rich class that will do anything to the rest of the world to hold onto what they have."

"And they'll also do anything to you and the rest of the workers."

"Only up to a point. They know we've got to be treated fairly well if we're going to do the work."

You couldn't get ahead of him.

"What about Communism?" I asked him. "They say knock off the rich and let the poor have it."

"Don't like their system at all," Jack said, shaking his head. "There's no way for a man to get ahead with them. It means everyone's a loser. For keeps."

He had an answer for everything.

He told me a lot about Arabella and her parents, too. He knew I'd been meeting her at Myrtle Grove.

"You was observed," he said with a shy sort of smile. "But we never said anything. You'd better watch out for her, though."

"How's that, Jack?"

"She's a witch . . . no, I'm just kidding. I don't know Miss Marlborough at all, they've only been on the property since their own house burned down about a year ago. But I know Bert Halca, who was their super when they had their own place, over on Packenback Road. Just him and one other man to help in the summers. Not a big place, but nice. I think Mr. Marlborough was better off then. Anyhow . . . you won't get sore if I tell you?"

"No, go ahead."

"It's nothing against her, just that sometimes people are sensitive. Well, Bert was with them from before she was born, so he really knew her, and it was a small place, the kind where a kid is always around the men who are working there. He claims she used to tell him when she was real little—only about six—that Mr. and Mrs. Marlborough weren't her real parents. She said she had no parents, that she was the daughter of a witch who came around and talked to her and gave her tips on what to do to get even with people. Bert said a lot of kids say things like that, but she could scare him, a grown man, with it because she was so intense. And so many details.

"But she had a tough time, too. The Marlboroughs fought all the time—he fought, and she was on the receiving end, Bert says—and then there were terrible battles between old Mrs. Marlborough and her son, Miss Marlborough's father. When that old lady came out to visit she used to get him going so he'd break down and cry."

"Like Mr. Revere."

"Oh, much worse, to hear Bert tell it. Those rich old ladies can really put it to their sons. And there have been a lot of fights since they came here. Miss Marlborough had a hard time. But that business about the witch . . . isn't that where the word 'bewitching' comes from?"

"I don't know. Maybe."

"Because that's what Bert used to say about her—she was 'bewitching.' Well, she is very beautiful, the face that sank a thousand ships, or whatever the song says."

I didn't say anything. He had a way of making the most casual remark seem to have hidden meanings, and I was trying not to miss anything he said.

"Bert comes over to see them," he went on, "and she told him last summer she was going to marry Mr. Lochmann. 'That'll be a meeting of the evil eyes,' Bert says. 'Werewolves, watch out. You're no match for those two.'"

"Is Lochmann considered bewitching, too?"

"He's a very strange man. You never know where you are with him. But I wouldn't say he was bewitching. He's more a pervert, like."

"A pervert?" I was surprised at the word.

"I shouldn't have said that," Jack said, and he wouldn't explain why he'd said it in the first place.

"I talk too much," were his last words. "I'll bewitch myself if I don't stop. And maybe you, too. Have to watch out for that, don't think anyone wants to be bewitched . . . "

22

I WOKE UP EARLY THE NEXT MORNING, because they don't let you sleep. They get you up for breakfast whether you want it or not. I didn't, but I ate it. No seconds, though. Jack and I didn't talk much, just sat around waiting for something to happen. The place was so hot you felt sleepy all the time.

Jack got out first. A Waterlukker lawyer posted bond, and the turnkey came and opened up for him.

"Well, Ox," he said, "somebody loves me up there."

"One of those wonderful people at the top," I said.

"One of those," he said, nodding his head. "Listen, they'll be letting you out soon, too."

I could tell he was upset because he'd gotten out before me.

"You're the backbone of the country, Jack," I told him. "I didn't know there were any left like you."

He wanted to shake hands but didn't want to be pushy, so I put mine through the bars and he grabbed it.

"No," he said, "it's you—you and the other people who have it—who are the real backbone of this country. If we didn't have you people, we'd be like every other country."

"And we wouldn't want that."

The guard was kind of intrigued and annoyed at the same time.

"Come on," he said to Jack, "let's go."

Jack waved and his face kind of worked for a minute. Then he started off. He was almost out of sight when he yelled back, "I had to hit you!"

"I get it!" I hollered after him. It didn't seem to make much difference anymore.

He was all right, Jack Taffle. What I'd told him was true—there aren't many like him. I lay there and thought how sad it was that he'd live all his life in poverty and be buried in a cheap box and no one would ever care, or even know he'd lived. So many millions have done it that way in this country. And all over the world. Billions. And for what?

They let me out about an hour later. Dad and Bones Blossom were in the waiting room, along with Mr. Farnsworth. They weren't saying much and we went out to the car. It was even colder than the day before and still cloudy.

"I thought there was supposed to be a hearing," I said.

"They waived it," Mr. Farnsworth said.

"They've caved in," Bones said to me then. "The possibility of publicity was too much and they . . . "

But I wasn't looking at him, I was looking at Dad. He was driving and had his eyes on the road. Finally he looked at me.

"OK," he said. "We went up there last night." Bones stopped talking. "They have caved in, Bones is right. He can tell you about it later. So we didn't have any trouble getting in. Or getting to see her. I told her we were . . . well, winners, or whatever, and that she could come with us. She said . . . she said she didn't want to. Ox, I tried and Sally did, too. Everything we could think of. She says she wants to stay there."

"Has she really cracked up?"

Dad looked at me hard. "She doesn't look the same, Ox. She's calm, but she seems a little crazy."

"Did they do anything to her? Injections? Or shock treatments?"

"They say not. The doctors there swear she was like that when she was brought in."

"Did he do anything? Or can you tell?"

"We talked to him before we went up," Dad said. "He swears he didn't do anything, either. Half admits that he would have tried to if she'd resisted, but claims she went with him quietly that morning. She told Sally the same thing, that no one has coerced her. Andy did say she was different that morning than she'd been when she came in the night before."

"How?"

"I gather that she was her usual self at night, bouncing around. He and Lizzie had already cooked Kensington up for her, and he was wondering how he'd swing it. But the next morning there was no problem. If he's telling the truth, it doesn't make sense."

"No, it doesn't."

"I hated to leave her there," he said, "but we couldn't drag her out. Go up and try yourself. You can take the chopper."

"I've got to have some breakfast first," I said. "Then I'll go." The meals I'd had in jail had left me starved.

Then Bones and Mr. Farnsworth gave me the details on the rest of it. I listened because I wanted to know everything that had happened. When the Waterlukker lawyers and publicity experts and Mr. Revere found out from the newspapers that the story was going to break the next morning, they had a conference. Three of the Waterlukker brothers and a dozen of their lawyers and all Mrs. Revere's lawyers and a lot of other experts came out to Myrtle Grove. "Chopper landing every five minutes," Bones said and Mr. Farnsworth nodded. "The others were flying holding patterns. It looked like the evacuation of Saigon. In reverse, I guess.

"Their lawyers and PR experts always feel that any legal fuss the Waterlukkers get into creates bad publicity. They're so powerful that the public always feels they're bullying whomever they're having a fight with. Even if they win, they lose. So the point is to keep out of court.

"When you boil this situation down, it's got bad publicity written all over it. A kid gets hit with a shovel—incidentally, that bandage needs a hairdresser—and another kid gets put in the booby hatch. Sorry, but that is where she is. Anyhow, those are the human facts. In rebuttal, we have some weak hot air about trespassing and holding up butlers and gardeners by their shirts, and tossing the guy with the shovel into a tree. But those misdemeanors don't balance the human interest side—let's face it, they don't come close. Can you imagine the laughter and curiosity? Who is this kid who can throw grown men into trees, et cetera?"

Bones started to laugh, and then he choked and waved Mr. Farnsworth to go on, and he did. "From a strictly legal standpoint, they might have had the upper hand. You were trespassing when you were hit, and Arabella Marlborough is a . . . family problem. That's what Mrs. Revere kept saying. I wasn't there, but a colleague who was . . . has briefed me. They kept trying to explain to Mrs. Revere that having the upper hand in the eyes of the law might have been . . . er, viable if she weren't a Waterlukker. But because she is, it wasn't. She couldn't be persuaded to understand, and it took the combined efforts of her husband and brothers and half the New York bar to make her see the light. She finally did."

Then they had called Mr. Farnsworth at Severn House and offered to drop all charges if we'd do the same and not discuss it with the newspapers any more. He consulted with Dad, and called them back to tell them Big Andy would have to let Arabella go. Big Andy didn't fight very hard on that one—"How could he, with all that artillery looking at him?" Bones said—and so it was settled.

"She'll become a ward of court," Mr. Farnsworth said. He seemed a lot sharper than he had the day before. "For practical purposes, it means that she can . . . well . . . " He looked at Dad.

"Become something like a relation of mine," Dad said. "Of ours, I should say. When we got that out of them last night I naturally thought it was all settled."

"You did some job," I said.

"It fell into our hands," Mr. Farnsworth said with a slight cough.

I was thinking about it, to keep from thinking about other things. "But they still had the problem of the newspapers, didn't they?" I asked Mr. Farnsworth.

"In what way?"

"You'd let the papers have the story—they could still print it."

"Oh, no. Once the Waterlukker side had the agreement with us, they were home free there. They just turned the papers off."

"How could they do that?"

"Well, it was abortive. It didn't really come to legal warfare. So it wasn't that much of a story. And they have friends on the papers. They can apply pressure. If it had been a political or economic story involving one of the brothers, they couldn't have stopped it even if it *was* suddenly stillborn. But a minor incident—almost a gossip column item—involving the sister, who isn't in politics or finance . . . what's that? So the papers didn't mention it. And never will. But I stress the fact that the incident was quashed between the interested parties— that's what made the difference."

"What if they hadn't been able to turn the papers off?"

"Then they would have figured they had nothing to lose, gone back on their agreement with us, and geared for a real fight."

"Nice honest people," Bones said.

I was thinking of Jack Taffle. He knew what they were really like, better than anyone. He only wanted to get there himself. Not really, that was a joke he had.

"Realists," Mr. Farnsworth said. He admired them.

"They're cheap," Dad said. "The whole bunch. No style at all."

Mr. Farnsworth looked puzzled at that, but he didn't say anything. We were almost at the house then, and when we got there I headed right for the kitchen.

Carmen fixed me a gigantic breakfast, and I put every bit of it away. She and Hans kept staring at me and I asked them what the matter was.

"Oh, to spend a night in jail!" Carmen wailed. "A nice boy like you."

"You were not being scared?" Hans asked.

"What of? They don't beat you. Actually, I had a good rest. And a pleasant talk with Jack Taffle."

"Jack was being there? Oh, yes, they told me he was. In the same cell? You was working on him for what he did?"

"He's not bad, Hans. No, I didn't do anything to him."

Ted came in then and was very quiet. Things had gotten way past what he understood. I could tell he thought he was in the middle of a war or something.

After breakfast I cleaned up. Sally wanted me to go to the doctor and have a new bandage put on, but I said there wasn't time. So she made me sit in a chair while she cut off some of the dirtiest parts and wrapped it with clean gauze and put on fresh tape.

"It's some beehive," she said. "Looks like you've had it on since Labor Day."

"I almost feel as if I have."

"Want me to come with you?"

"I thought about it, and I'd say . . . negative. You saw her last night, and if it didn't work then . . . well, what could you do today?"

"You're right, I was just offering . . . we really tried, Ox."

"Dad told me."

"She was a different person. Not in a big way, but . . .

it seemed more a question of difference in emphasis. She was calm, and very definite when she said she didn't want to leave. If you'd been meeting her for the first time, you wouldn't have thought she was . . . "

"Sally, *why* doesn't she want to leave? Does she say?"

"No. She just says she's comfortable there, and she wants to stay. We tried everything we could think of. 'You're perfectly all right, why do you want to stay in an institution? You can get away from Big Andy for good now. Don't you want to see Ox?' And all she'd say was that she didn't want to leave."

"Did she say how long she wanted to stay?"

"We asked her if she wanted to be there forever, and she would only say, 'I'll see.' "

"Dad said she seemed a little crazy. You say she seemed all right, at least to someone seeing her for the first time."

"I think he must have meant a little crazy compared to what she was . . . "

"Sally, I don't get it. I'm going up there blind."

"I don't get it either, Ox."

"If it's something coming at her from outside, I can help her. Even from inside if I can understand it. But something from inside that I can't understand . . . then I don't know."

"She may be all right today. She may be back to normal. Wait until you see her."

"Thanks for everything."

"I didn't make your father go," she said quickly. "He wanted to. He laid it on the line for you, Ox. He told Bones and Sam Farnsworth that he'd go all the way against the Waterlukkers. When we flew up to New

Haven last night, he was a different man. Committed. A committed man, Ox."

"I've never seen him like this, either," I told her. "But he's doing it for himself, Sally. Yes, partly for me, but mostly for himself."

"He likes you," she said stubbornly. "He respects you."

I could see it from her angle, but she hadn't known Dad as long as I have.

23

DAD'S HELICOPTER PILOT was waiting for me and we took right off. I hate the noise they make, but helicopters can get you around a metropolitan area in a hurry. By car it was about seventy-five miles to New Haven, and took nearly two hours through the traffic. With the helicopter you went right across Long Island Sound and were there in twenty minutes.

The pilot had been across the night before and knew where to go. We came down on the grounds inside the walls, not more than a hundred yards from the administration building. There was an icy wind and it felt like snow was coming.

"The people here bitched last night about landing inside," he said, "but where else am I going to put down? I'll wait for you. Any idea how long?"

"No."

He nodded as though that was what he expected.

"Your father told me to wait," he said. "Take your time."

An idea came into my head. "How soon could we get out of here if we had to?"

"That's what your old man asked me last night," he

said, grinning. He had wide spaces between his teeth, and reminded me of a kid I knew in Palm Beach. I couldn't remember the kid's name, though. "If I see you coming in a hurry, I'll hit the switches and be ready to go by the time you get to the door."

I could tell that's what he wanted to do. "That means you'll have to wait out here. It's pretty cold for that."

"I've got lined boots." He stamped his feet. "And a thermos of coffee. Besides, that's what I'm paid for." He grinned again, and I knew that Dad had given him something extra. Probably a hundred.

Inside the administration building, the reception desk was in the middle of a large room with a lot of hallways leading off it. It had a high ceiling and there was a big Christmas tree in one corner. The woman at the desk asked me how I'd gotten in, because I had no gate pass. When I said by helicopter, she thought I was a patient—the bandage had something to do with it, too—and called for a Dr. Prager. He wasn't so bad, and we got things straightened out, and he took me to the reception room where I'd meet Arabella. It had an oval table and chairs in it, like a small model of those conference rooms they have in businesses.

I sat there for quite a while before Arabella came in. She was dressed in her own clothes—a dark skirt and a white blouse—and she looked all right.

"Hello, Ox." She sat down sort of across from me. "How are you?"

"I'm fine."

"I hear you had a night behind bars." She smiled a small smile. "Sorry it was on my behalf. How was it?"

"Not bad. I had Jack Taffle to keep me company."

"That must have been nice."

"We got along all right—he's sort of interesting."

I was feeling my way. She looked all right, and she still had a sense of humor. She seemed like herself, except that there was no carryover from the way we'd been a couple of days before. It was as though that was wiped out. And she gave that impression of being from a long time ago. I'd felt it before, but now it was so much stronger. It was in the way she sat and moved and spoke. It was hard to pin down, but it was real.

"You're wondering where I went," she said, with that way she had of knowing what you were thinking. "I'm still here. At least part of me is. I don't forget our afternoon at the Morville. I never could. I'll remember what we talked about . . . sitting in your lap at the end, everything . . . for the rest of my life."

"I'm glad—I couldn't forget it either, and wouldn't want to."

"Your father and Sally didn't understand that . . . well, how could they, since they weren't there? But they couldn't have understood anyhow. They think people are either all one way or all another. They don't realize that any of us can be several ways at the same time. I hope you understand that."

"Not quite, not right this moment. But I'll work on it."

"When I left you, life seemed like heaven." She leaned forward a little, but that was all. "I went home on a cloud. There wasn't even much trouble with Big Andy. A certain amount of grumble, a certain amount of 'We'll settle this in the morning.' But nothing wild, nothing drastic. So I was still in the same mood when I went to bed. Until I woke about four o'clock, and . . . it wasn't that I started 'thinking,' Ox, it was more that thoughts started washing over me, like waves at the beach. They were from different angles, but they had the same message: what we decided—that I'd go back for a year or so and then get out—was too vague. I had to get out right away. But most important, *I* had to do something. I had to stop letting other people do things for me."

"But things have changed since we talked," I said. "The day before yesterday it was either go on your own or stay at home. Now there's another choice. You're going to become a ward of the court, which means you could practically be a member of our family, such as it is."

"But that would just be sponging in a new way, don't you see?"

"No, but I'll leave it for the moment."

"In the night I was thinking of how self-indulgent I am, and always have been. I'd been practically marrying myself to you . . . Me! A girl who has no more sense of responsibility than a . . . gnat. It was the silliest performance of my life. What I have to do is make something out of myself. I . . . "

"You already are something."

"What? A charming nitwit."

"Charm is rare. And you're more than charming. You have character."

"If I do, it's undeveloped."

"But why does it have to develop here, in an institution?"

"Oh, I don't know that I'll stay here. Or that they'll let me. But I want to be in hard places. I have to be. I couldn't get on my feet in the bosom of the Olmstead family. You're all so much stronger than I am. I'd always be a cripple. I have to stay on my own, in hard places, until I'm not a cripple."

I shook my head. "You're not a cripple now."

"Listen to me—I do pathetic things. I hear Sally say 'Negative' for 'No' and five minutes later I'm doing it myself."

"I didn't hear you."

"I managed to hold myself in check around you. But I shouldn't *have* to. I shouldn't be so compulsive. I have to get over it."

"That's so minor," I said. "It doesn't make you a cripple."

"There's worse," she said. "Well, maybe I'm not a cripple down deep, but I am on top. I've got to do something about that."

Her hands stayed in her lap, she wasn't using them at all.

"If you leave here, where will you go?"

"I don't know—some other hard place. Perhaps a convent. Don't look so shocked. Remember, I told you I liked the religious atmosphere."

"I remember, but that's not exactly the same as going in for good." I thought then I had to say something to shake her up. "Besides, how can you go to a convent? I hear you used to call yourself a witch."

"Who told you that?"

"Jack Taffle, from Bert Halca."

"I was an infant then," she said. "I wish I *were* a witch—evil and efficient like Lizzie—but I'm such a duffer. Listen, it doesn't matter so much where I go. The important thing is that I'm not going to think all the time about what *I* am going to do. I'm going to take it as it comes. The new order began yesterday morning. When Big Andy said he was going to take me up to the main house, I went. When I got there, he and Lizzie had a few shrinks from here to examine me. The old Arabella would have jumped through the window, gotten to a phone, called Ox, gotten rescued, et cetera, et cetera . . . all to prove what? I'd be the same, just off on another adventure. No, I have to change inside.

"So I just talked quietly with the doctors. That was rather amusing, because they were all primed for the old Arabella, and the leap through the window. Didn't know quite what to say when I said I'd do whatever they wanted. Went outside and conferenced with Big Andy. 'She doesn't seem too nuts . . . maybe she's not.' But they were in too deep then, and Big Andy told them to go all the way or lose the Waterlukker grant, and Lizzie drew a few lines under the ultimatum. So they came back in and certified me, and off we went.

"And do you know, I was actually lighthearted when I got in the car with them. I felt as though I was taking the right first step for the first time in my life. I was hitting bottom, of course I was, but isn't that the place you have to get before you can start back?"

"I thought marrying Lochmann was hitting bottom. You called it the worst thing you could think of."

"Too spectacular. And too selfish. Marrying for money, even if someone else gets the money—Big Andy in that case—has too many loose ends. This is clean and neat and hard."

"But what do they think of you here? Don't they know you're all right?"

"Sure. So they don't give me any trouble."

"But now that the Waterlukkers have caved in . . . "

"Oh, the order came immediately from Big Andy—let her go. But I told Dr. Oliver . . . have you met him?"

I shook my head. "Negative."

"Don't tease. I hope you do meet him before you leave—not a bad old duck. Anyhow, I told him that it was so sudden, letting me go. Here I was just settling down for a rest I was convinced I needed, and I get chucked out. He hemmed and hawed, but when he figured out that the bills would be paid anyhow he said I could stay."

"Doesn't that go against your new idea of taking things as they come?"

"You mean they said I could go, and I'm staying?"

"Uh-huh."

"I can't rationalize everything perfectly. They put me here, and so I shouldn't leave until I've run the experience through. It's rather interesting, too, being with all these nuts. Don't worry, I won't stay forever. When I feel I've had enough, and when something pushes me— don't ask me what—I'll leave. When I can go from here to another place where I can be alone to keep working on . . . myself."

She was talking as though she didn't care what I thought of what she was saying, but then she shot me a sort of anxious look. I didn't say anything for a little while and neither did she.

"Do you want my opinion?" I finally asked her.

"Of course I do."

"I think it's a lot of hot air."

Her face fell a little.

"Arabella, you're in a nuthouse and you're not nuts.

You can talk all you want, but you can't get by that. It doesn't make sense, it's hot air."

Her eyes hardened a little.

"I told you the other day that you're all right at bottom, that I'd bet on you, and you said that was all you needed. Remember that?" I said it in the closest and quietest way I could, trying to reach inside her to where she really was.

"I do remember it," she said slowly. "I told you I'd never forget anything we said that day."

"If that was all you needed, why do you need this?"

"I don't know. I can't be held to . . . " She stopped. I could tell she realized she was going back on something important.

"Can't you? You didn't say that was enough only to me, you were saying it to yourself, too. Now you're going back on something you promised yourself."

Her head was down. "I know it," she said in a whisper. "I know it. But I can't help it." She put her head up, and her eyes were wet. "I can't help it, Ox."

I didn't say anything.

"I didn't mean to tell you this, but my real flaw came to me the other night."

She stopped, but I still didn't say anything. Ordinarily I would have said something like "Not another one," but this wasn't the time for that kind of remark. I knew she had to be handled very gently.

"It's one of the worst flaws. A Grand Canyon of a flaw. I need diversions."

More silence.

"That doesn't sound so bad when you first hear it— who doesn't need diversions? But my need is different from most people's. Everything is a diversion to me. Ideas, places, people . . . nothing lasts for more than a few days, a month or so. No, I can say it better than that. I can go along with ordinary things and people for any period of time. But once I get excited about something, once I build anything or anyone up, then the letdown has to come. Very soon after. I can't hold to anything once I'm really committed to it. Commitment means the end of the commitment. It just . . . slides away."

"Everything?" I asked her.

She understood that I was asking about the afternoon we had spent, and her feeling for me and all the rest.

"Yes, Ox." Her head was down again. "Everything." She looked up and the tears were starting down her cheeks. "Even you."

There was nothing I could say.

"Even everything we talked about . . . and meant. God knows I meant all of it. I never meant anything so much! That's what makes this . . . so awful."

I couldn't help it, the certainty that she was nuts went through me hard, and made me sore. No, I decided in the next moment, she wasn't nuts, but she'd do anything to take center stage. She couldn't be satisfied with what she had, fitting into what was possible. She had to do the big, wild thing, and set everyone on their ear. This was bigger and more of a mess than just walking away from her family and letting Dad take care of her, so she went for it.

I didn't know how to handle what was happening. If I came down on her hard for being an actress, it was what she expected, what she wanted. If I did nothing, then I missed the chance to kick her out of it. But could she be kicked out of it? I didn't know which way to go, so I waited. I was afraid that if I was hard on her and frightened her, she'd pull back and I'd lose all chance of reaching her.

"You think I'm exaggerating," she said. She always knew where you were.

"I think you're all right, but for some reason you've convinced yourself that you're not," I hedged.

"I'm not making it up. I *am* sick to the extent that I have this diversion problem. Don't you understand that I hate it, that it disgusts me? I don't want to go on living with it. I've got to get rid of it. Can you see that?"

I almost could. She'd changed again, and seemed honest and firm and right. As though she was standing outside and seeing herself and everything more clearly than anyone else could, including me.

"I can and I can't, at the same time."

"I owe you everything," she said. "I couldn't do this if I didn't know you."

"You mean if you didn't know me, you'd never have gotten here?"

"I wouldn't have had the guts," she said. "I'd be beating on some door somewhere, trying to run away from myself in some fresh adventure."

"My head is beginning to spin," I said. "Because you know me, you can walk away. Is that it?"

"Something like that."

Suddenly it made me sore. "Why didn't you call me yesterday morning?"

"I didn't have a chance . . . oh, why not be honest. I could have, somehow. I didn't . . . because—well, I suppose because it would have been like jumping through the window. I never could have explained that in five minutes, though, so what was the point?"

The point was that I was waiting, I thought to myself. It was on the tip of my tongue to say to her, "You'll never make it if you don't make those key phone calls," as a joke because of all the times she'd kidded me about not making it. I couldn't say it, though, and I had to face the hardest fact—jokes were finished, we weren't going to have any more. That's when I knew it was really bad, when I knew I couldn't be natural with her anymore.

"I guess there was no point," I said. If you can't talk naturally to someone you like it doesn't matter much what you say. But I went through the motions. "You were talking about diversions—how do you know this isn't just one more?"

"I know because it doesn't excite me. There's no up, so there won't be a down." She stood up, and I thought she was going and I felt terrible and there was nothing I could do or say. Anything would have been wrong.

But she didn't go. She knew how I felt and wanted to do something about it.

She smiled at me, and then came and knelt beside the chair I was in and took my hands. "I know that when you walk out of here, you'll cross me off in a matter of hours. I know that, Ox. But even when you do, remember it as it was—at the Morville and here, this minute. Especially now, when you believe a little bit—I know you do—that I am all right, and that I'm doing the right thing.

"Listen, I do everything off you, don't you know that, you big creep? I'm doing this because of you. I want to make myself right in your eyes, don't you get it? I thought you knew something about girls."

226

Her eyes were shining and she seemed like she'd been before.

"I never thought I knew too much, and now I think it's zero," I said.

"Gruff bear," she said. "Gruffest bear in the valley. Much more a bear than an ox, by the way. And gruff with reason, because . . . this kangaroo, Arabella A., has been jumping all over his honeypots, crying, 'I want to improve myself until you can be proud of me, Bear.' I don't blame you, to you it's all just hot air and self-indulgence. But to me it's important. I want to be all right. For myself and for you. But I can't get all right leaning on you. I have to do it on my own. If I make it . . . I'll put up my jumping feet forever. I'll be the quietest, most docile 'roo you've ever seen."

She looked wonderful and she seemed very sure of herself.

"I'm not asking you to 'wait'—but I'm sure you understand that. Gruff bears, golden oxen, people like that don't wait. I know it. That's the chance I take. But I have to take it."

She made it all sound so reasonable. And tempting. I could feel it in my chest.

"I know it's putting the pressure on you," she said. "Not on me, really, but on you. I know I seem like an irresponsible butterfly, and that you have to worry about me. I know how unfair that is. But it's still fairer than if I became a 'member of the Olmstead family, such as it is,' and pretended everything was fine. That would be worse. I can't explain it beyond there."

She got to her feet. "Now I have to go." She smoothed her skirt in the way she had. "We could talk all day, but we'd be going downhill. Everything's been said."

I stood up, too, and she came and kissed me. I held her and she kept her head close against me. "I'll be in touch with you," she whispered. "If . . . you know." I could barely hear her. "Don't come to me or let anyone else come, please. . . . I have to go now. If I stay here, I'll fall apart. I love you." She pushed back slightly against my arms and I let her go. Then she came close again and said, "Never think later that if you'd done anything differently it would have turned out another way. I can't stand to think of you torturing yourself that way. You could kidnap me—I saw the chopper—and I'd probably go with you without a struggle . . . I'm close to it now . . . but I'd get away again, because I have to do this."

Then she pushed away again and I let her go again, and this time she left the room without turning around. The last I saw of her was her back, so straight, and her beautiful hair, and the swing of her clothes, and her long skinny legs.

What she had done at the end was what she always did. I had been wondering while I was holding her if I shouldn't grab her and take her with me. I had the feeling that I was wrong either way—to take her or leave her—and the uncertainty was making me sick. She sensed that, the way she always sensed everything, and she made it all right for me. It wouldn't last, I knew, but it would get me out and on the way.

Even while I had the feeling that later I'd think I hadn't done the right thing or hadn't done enough, I couldn't get past straight admiration for her. She was all wrong, I suppose, but she was perfect at it. I could hardly take it in, but she had made me think we had a bond between us that was bigger than the one we'd had at the Morville. At the end, she'd done what she always did—left me with the feeling that we'd gone further, further toward some . . . I can't explain it in words. We never went backward. Even when it looked desperate, it was always ahead.

With all she could do, that power of making you think you were always going further was what did it to you the most. No matter how often she used it, you still couldn't hold out against it, even if you wanted to. And it was a contradiction, like everything about her. She could seem like the most selfish and self-centered person in the world, and then you found out that it was always you who walked away with something. You never left Arabella empty-handed.

She'd done it so well that I was actually almost feeling all right when I walked out of the place. Dr. Oliver, the one she'd mentioned, came up to me near the door and asked if there was any way he could help.

"Arabella said you were a special friend," he said. He was old, with hair growing out of his ears, but very nice. You could tell that.

"I don't think there's anything," I said. "I suppose you know she's perfectly all right, but she has her own reasons for wanting to be here."

"Yes, she's perfectly all right," he repeated, looking at me. Most old people talk all the time, but he was quiet, as though he was waiting for something.

I finally got it that he thought I could tell him why she wanted to be there.

So I told him I didn't know why, but that she was not a fool or a phony.

"Will you let her stay until she wants to leave?" I asked

229

him. I meant would he let her stay off faith, I guess that's the word.

I think he understood it that way, because he said, "I would say that she should not be here, but it's so unusual . . . I have agreed to it."

He hadn't met Dad the night before, so I gave him our address in Locust Valley and in Palm Beach. "We'll do anything," I said.

"That's good to know," he said. He'd gotten what he wanted and he looked relieved. I should have stayed longer—I knew he wanted to ask me about her—but I couldn't.

He took both my hands in his to say good-bye. He was very nice, and he acted as though he knew a lot.

Outside, the pilot was walking around near the helicopter. When he saw me, he jumped in and started it. He had the door open and was ready to go when I got there.

"There's no hurry," I yelled at him over the engines.

"I wish there were," he said, and I didn't know how much he knew about what was going on.

We took off and I tried to keep from looking down at the place, but I couldn't. It was spread out below us, and Arabella was in it, and the reaction set in and I felt lousy.

24

I COULDN'T THINK STRAIGHT GOING BACK, so I didn't try. I knew Dad and Sally would be waiting for some kind of explanation, and I concentrated on what I'd tell them. What Arabella had said didn't make a lot of sense when you thought of telling it to Dad. But he had put plenty in on everything, and so had Sally, and I decided they deserved a straight story whether it made sense or not. And a straight story was what I gave them, minus the personal stuff between Arabella and me.

"You mean she's saying something like 'It's a far, far better thing I do'?" Dad asked at the end.

"Something like that," I said.

"What do you think, Ox?" Sally asked me.

"I don't know. I don't know whether she's just an actress who wants center stage or whether she really believes she's doing something that's honest and right—for herself, anyhow. Or whether what she's doing *is* right for her, no matter what she believes."

"I liked her from the beginning," Dad said slowly, building himself a drink. "From the time she did that lousy Bacall imitation and then turned it into something amusing. But I have to say I don't like this."

"It's her problem, though," Sally said.

"Not altogether," Dad said. "We all worked like hell to get her out. Out of Andy's and then out of Kensington. We took on those Waterlukkers and came out on top. We ought to be celebrating, having a good time, with her as part of that good time. She knows that, she's sensitive. But she wouldn't let it happen that way. No, she had to do something she knew would throw a wet blanket over everything. She spoiled the party."

Dad can't say a worse thing about anyone than that they spoiled the party.

"I'm sure that wasn't her intention," Sally said, with just a touch of sarcasm.

"Wasn't it?" Dad asked her. "Ox himself said he doesn't know whether she's an actress or not. I say she is and that she knew what she was doing all along. She wanted to tie us in knots!"

He had a point—that it was possible—and Sally and I both knew it.

"I say we can't be sure," Sally said. "That's what Ox said, and he's right."

"You can't live with uncertainty," Dad said. "No one can. You come down on one side or the other of everything whether you like it or not. Everyone has to."

He was right there, too.

Dad came down on actress, and that made him so mad he got drunk that night for the first time since we came there. Sally stuck with uncertainty, and she got drunk with him. I stayed with uncertainty, too, and went to bed miserable. Arabella had done it to all of us.

The next day was the day before Christmas, and Dad didn't go to New York, but just grumped around the place with a hangover. A couple of times he was on the

232

verge of going over it again with me, I could tell. He hated mysteries and he hated uncertainty, and above all he hated people who got him into those things. At the moment he had it in for Arabella, but I knew it wasn't going to take him too long to switch from her to me, because I was around and I was the one who had brought her in. Dad was good while there was a quick, clear-cut fight, but he fell apart when it took a lot of time and got complicated.

Sally was down, too, but for a different reason. She'd made a real effort to pull herself together since we'd come up from Palm Beach because Dad had pulled himself together. Sally had seen a lot in life, and she didn't believe in much. So when Dad got depressed, she went down with him. She couldn't hold out alone. Maybe she wasn't so wrong.

It was like the calm before the storm that day. They both got up late, and Dad had a beer with breakfast, which was always a bad sign, and she had some wine. They were restless, and went out for lunch.

"I told you she'd cause trouble," Dad said to me before they left. "I guaranteed it. Do you remember that?" His eyes were little and red and he was spoiling for a fight.

I told him I did remember him saying that, and he shook his head in disgust as he left.

Hans and Carmen had to be told something when they asked, so I said Arabella was fine and would be leaving Kensington soon.

"But why she was there?" Hans asked. "That was a booby hutch. She was having no need to have been going in a booby hutch."

"She needs a rest," I said. "She wasn't feeling well."

"Why not rest in a house?" Carmen asked. "Here she could be. Why not?"

"She didn't want to be a burden."

"Your father was upset," Hans said. "He was angry with me about Christmas but I was telling that it was about that girl."

"Hans only said it was too bad there was no tree in the living room, the way we used to have," Carmen said, "and that made him angry."

"He was saying he'd rather he was wrestling with a vulture than look at a Christmas tree," Hans said. "He said it was being silly, and if I said more he was making a tree out of me. He was not saying those things like a joke. He was being very angry."

"He was upset," I said. I knew it was terrible to them that there was no tree in the living room. Arabella on top of that had been too much.

"Mrs. Sally was upset, I know," Carmen said. "I asked her this morning what had happened and she wouldn't talk about it. That's why we have to ask you."

"Yes," I said, "she's very fond of Arabella. Both she and my father are."

"And you, too, Ox," Carmen said. "You are very fond of her, too."

"That's right," I said. "We're all upset."

"Hans and I are," Carmen said.

"She was a lovely girl," Hans said.

They were standing in front of me in the dining room where I was having lunch, Carmen twisting the cords of her apron and Hans with his hands behind his back. They did care, for me if for nobody else, and what was happening at a Christmas with no tree was too much.

234

They wanted me to say something to cheer them up, but I didn't have it. Their being upset was just another load for me, and I wanted them to go away.

They finally did, and I finished up my lunch. Everything was spoiled—I couldn't even look at *Hunting the Hunters* without it reminding me of . . . a lot of things. And making me wonder just what its final message was.

After lunch I went into the sunken living room and sat in front of the fire. I couldn't think of anything else to do. I hadn't been there for more than five minutes when Ted came down the steps and flopped into a chair across from me.

"I hear everything worked out," he said in a cheerful way.

"Pretty well," I said.

"Except that I gather—no one will really talk to me anymore—that Arabella is staying on at Kensington, and nobody knows why." His English accent was light to moderate.

He wanted me to explain, but I wasn't going to tell him anything. Dad and Sally had put something in, so they deserved to be talked to. Besides, they cared—they wouldn't have gotten drunk if they didn't. So did Hans and Carmen, Nazis or not. But Ted didn't care, he was just curious. He was like most people, there was nothing inside him at all. Nothing but curiosity. He had to live through or off the ones who did care, when he could find them, the way most people do. He was just like those people who are always reading about Jackie and the Kennedys. What they call the great majority.

I had liked Ted at the beginning. I had even thought of making it up to him in some way for being such a lousy student. But I didn't like him much anymore and I wasn't going to make anything up to him. He didn't deserve it.

"Why shouldn't she be there?" I asked him. "She's nuts, isn't she?"

He almost jumped out of his chair. "Do you think so? I thought you were quite . . . of the opposite opinion."

"They say so at Kensington, and how can all those doctors be wrong?"

"You don't believe in doctors. I know that."

"I've been persuaded."

"No, it's something else. I wonder if . . ."

He went on talking but I didn't listen. I hadn't handled it very well. I wanted to turn him off, but I'd been too sarcastic. I'd muffed it and now all I wanted was to get away. So I told him I was taking a walk, and left him there.

As I went down from the house, I remembered the night Arabella had muffed it with him and Sally had covered for her, and I had explained to her afterward how she should have handled it. I felt the back of my neck get red when I thought of explaining things to Arabella. She must have smiled at that.

Don't be sarcastic, I told myself. That isn't the answer, either.

I wandered through the woods, along the path where I had gone to meet her so many times. It had been fall then, and now it was winter.

Finally I came to the gate. The padlock, which had been open for so many weeks, was closed through the chain. The gate was locked. They must have done that after Jack hit me, I thought, and I haven't been back since. It was only a few days, but it felt like a year.

It doesn't matter, I told myself, you weren't going through it anymore anyhow. I leaned my head against one of the iron posts. It was so cold that the skin on my forehead almost stuck to it, but it felt good.

Idle stuff ran through my head . . . It had been a heavy talk at Kensington—the heaviest—but she hadn't said anything about not getting heavy, or not making a big thing out of it. Probably no one did when things were really heavy, really big. And her hands had been quite still, too, except at the very end. But not much movement even then.

It's worse than if you were dead, I said, as though I was talking to her. If you were dead, even if you'd done it yourself, it would be a clean end, and we could all go on. But this way we can't. Nothing can move.

She had said she knew that what she was doing would put the pressure on me, that she knew how unfair it was. You have no idea how much pressure, I said, as though she could hear me, no idea how unfair. For someone who wanted nothing but comfort, it's a severe test. You've put the load on the old Ox, all right. Right from the beginning, I guess—poor old Ox, under pressure he will always defend the weak, but when peace is restored he wonders if it was worth it.

I had tried to be logical about it, sort it out. On one side was her flimsy story of why she wanted to stay at Kensington, why she had turned her back on me and everyone else. Her saying herself that she was only a socialite, especially in a pinch, cowardly and a herd animal, and not the aristocrat she seemed, able to stand alone. Bert Halca's unattractive stories of her as a child —not the witch part, but that she had gone under to her parents' troubles, cracked up, and run around making threats. Acting like Lizzie's granddaughter. Maybe she was.

On the other side, all her charm and honesty about so many things, her clean beauty, most of all her warmth, her wonderful softness. The rightness in her that was more than in anyone I'd ever known. Or would ever know, I had begun to believe.

And in the middle, the questions. Unfair, maybe, but they were there. Like . . . she had said she'd gone out to the place where we met even when she knew I wasn't going to be there. I believed that when she told me, but could I believe it now? Was she only like other girls, who said things like that to make you notice them? And even if she had come, was it because of me? Or . . . just part of making it all work out to this? If you looked at it that way, I had made a fool of myself. I had been . . . bewitched . . . and by a witch who'd had anorexia. You didn't know whether to laugh or cry.

The most confusing question of all was her half promise that she would come back to the world someday, come back to me. Was that something I could believe or was it only a bait to get me to tie myself to nothing?

What bothered me more than anything else, and frightened me, too, was that I had bet she was all right. I had told her that and I had meant it. I'd never done anything like that before, so I didn't know what it meant if I had lost. How would I pay? I knew I'd have to pay if I was wrong, but how? By losing my confidence, by having been taken so completely that I'd never be able to depend on myself again? That would be the cruelest way to have to pay. That would finish me right off. Well, if that was it, I'd just have to take it.

She'd also said that when I walked out of that place I'd cross her off in a matter of hours. Because she'd said it, I'd been determined not to do it, but now I began to wonder. Not about crossing her off, but about wiping the memory of her out to take the pain and pressure off myself. I couldn't wait to see what would happen, as she'd said herself I couldn't. No one could live permanently with uncertainty, Dad was right. You had to come down to an opinion one way or the other and stick to it until . . . well, until something definite made you change it. But you couldn't stay with *no* opinion, always wondering would she or wouldn't she. No one could. Least of all someone with my problems.

"If you try to clear up a mystery, you always find it isn't worth it," she had said. "Isn't that your experience?" Well, I had failed to clear up the mystery about her and that wasn't worth it, either. It was worse than not being worth it—it was pure pain. You can't win either way with mysteries.

You have to leave it here in the woods, I said to myself. You can't walk back with it. You have to leave it by this fence.

The tears came to my eyes. Go ahead, I said to myself, now's the time to blubber. Do it once and get it over with.

Across the fence was where we'd had such good times . . . in the magic valley, the place she'd invented and which was so real when she talked about it that you didn't ever want to leave it. The trolls and giants and ogres and witches and lords and peasants and sheepherders . . . and, finally, the beautiful Arabella Anorexia herself. Lilies over water.

She was a dream, I told myself, just like everyone else in the magic valley. It doesn't mean she wasn't real—don't they say dreams can be more real than anything that happens to you in the day?—but she was real in a dream. Now the dream is over and she's gone. You have to face it. You always felt she was from another time, and now she's gone back to that time. For good. That's the dark part of her, of her strangeness, of her being bewitching, that she can go back, way, way back, and never return to this world again. You have to face it.

But I couldn't face it. The unfairness and the fact that she was still alive came over me. I could feel the wet on my face, and my hands tightened in the padlock chain until I could feel the posts give.

Go ahead, I told myself. Let it all come out now, for once and for all.

So I did. I'd never let go physically that way before—like most people with a lot of strength, I've always been afraid of letting it all out. But I'd never felt like that, either, and it had to come out some way.

I pulled back on the chain until the posts did start to bend. I was going to get the chain and padlock off if it killed me. The posts bent but they were too springy to break, so I looped my hands in the chain and turned it against them. It bit into my hands but I kept turning, using all the leverage in my shoulders and back. My fingers felt like they were going, but I kept turning. When you get like that, you don't care. I'd have turned until my hands dropped off, I was that far gone.

The chain snapped and the padlock flew off and my hands were still intact. Then I tore the gate off the hinges and started in on the chain link fence itself. I pulled back on it until the tension on the wire started bending the posts. When they started going I pulled more. That section went down and I went right to the next one. I could feel my coat split over my back and my head felt like it was coming off. I can't remember it from then on, or how long I was at it. All I know is that I pulled until I dropped, because when I came to myself again I was down on the ground. The sweat was still pouring off me and my heart was pounding.

I stayed there quite a while, until the chill started to come over me. The fence was a mess—yards of wire and posts were down—but I wasn't sorry about it.

Then I got up and walked away. I didn't feel good, but I felt better. And I knew I'd left it there. It was over, and I'd never go under to it again.

25

IT WAS CHRISTMAS EVE THAT NIGHT, and the place was just like any other American rich house. Except for the detail of the missing tree. Dad and Sally had called up a lot of people and were having a big party. It was the first one they'd given since we came to Long Island, and you might have thought it would be hard to get a lot of people there. But it wasn't. People, especially rich people, are always ready for a party. And no matter how many parties are going on, there always seem to be enough people with nothing to do for one more.

"It was all being on the spurs of the minute," Hans told me. "They were saying to me that they wanted a party, and I was saying Carmen and I couldn't do it, and your father was saying, 'Didn't expect you to, call a caterer.' That was one hard job to find a caterer on this day, but I did."

There were bartenders and maids and the same old catered food, and a string trio playing in the sunken living room, and somewhere between seventy-five and a hundred people. At eight o'clock they all looked healthy and well dressed, and were polite enough. By twelve there were about fifty left, and they were going downhill fast. I could see them from the upstairs landing. I went to bed then, but I knew that by two or three o'clock they'd be down to thirty, and those thirty would be in shreds. I'd seen it too many times.

The caterers came back early Christmas morning and cleaned up, so the place looked all right by the time the guests were out of bed and walking around.

Dad and Sally and the ones who'd spent the night went out to a punch party, and I took a car and drove to Montauk. That's at the end of Long Island, about a hundred miles east of where we were, and fairly deserted. There's a lighthouse there and a Coast Guard station. Even though it was Christmas Day and cold, there were quite a few people out there. Beyond Montauk Point is nothing, just ocean. It's the end of the line.

On the way back I stopped in Easthampton to see the house Dad owned there. I'd found out he inherited it from my grandfather—it had been the family summer place. But Dad never got around to using it and so it just stood empty. It wasn't run down or anything, and had a caretaker. I wanted to see it because I had nothing better to do, and for one other reason.

Most of the houses in Easthampton are made of shingles that are grayish and brownish, with white trim on the windows and doors. Ours was fairly big and the grounds were pretty large. The caretaker was there, but he couldn't seem to figure out who I was. He was about sixty and very slow.

"I thought the family's name was Ormstead," he said.

"No, Olmstead." He was paid by one of Dad's accountants and never saw our name on a check or anything. It was all done through a holding company, and had something to do with taxes.

243

He didn't quite believe I was who I was, but he let me in. The house had about twenty rooms, and they were all furnished, everything lying waiting under the dust covers.

When we passed one bedroom, I could see that the dust covers were off, and he said, "My daughter stays here sometimes. I didn't think anybody would mind."

"No, that's all right," I told him.

The furniture in that room was plain but comfortable, just about right for a summer house. It might have been Dad's bedroom when he was a kid.

The bed in the master bedroom was enormous under its cover. That was where my grandfather and grandmother had slept. It was hard to imagine them there.

It was dark when I got back to Severn House, and Dad and Sally were out. I ate early and went to a movie.

The next day there was a Christmas card from Mom, from somewhere up in the Andes. "Finally out of Argentina," it said. "Never make that mistake again." Her Christmas cards were always a little late.

From then on, things settled into a new rhythm. Dad spent less and less time in New York, and when he did go in he used the hydrofoil. He gave up the helicopter, and the pilot was sort of upset about it.

"I thought I was doing my job," he said. "And more."

"I guess he doesn't like heights anymore," I said.

He gave me a funny look, but he didn't say anything.

Sally sort of slipped back into her old ways, and we started to get inefficient. But no one seemed to care. She and Dad weren't drinking wildly, but it was steady and they both looked different.

The house was full of people all the time. Most of them I'd never seen, but some I had. Bones Blossom came often and drank a lot and got Hans to say dragon over and over. That was the big sport, getting Hans to say dragon. Everyone did it. Winston Lochmann was there quite a bit, too. He talked German with Hans and Carmen in a serious way, and giggled and was a little sinister with everyone else. He was always invited to the parties—people liked to meet the boob who'd lost all his money in painting—and never knew why. Big Andy showed up from time to time. Dad had decided to let him handle some investments after all.

Dad's manner toward me changed, too, back to the critical.

One day we were in the sunken living room alone and he told me there was a lot of excitement in working.

"Don't you agree?" he asked me.

"Sure," I said.

"That's how I take care of myself," he said. "Working." It was two o'clock in the afternoon and he was having a drink. "I'm not working at this moment," he said, "but I do when I need it. To take care of myself."

Dad did take care of himself, but he wasn't taking care of himself then. Especially the part that wasn't connected to protecting money.

I'd wanted to ask him to let Jack Taffle be the caretaker at the Easthampton house—that was the reason I'd gone there—but I could tell I couldn't do anything with him, so I never brought it up.

He was getting more nervous all the time, and I wondered how long he was going to stick it out.

It was Ted's quitting that did it. There wasn't much

fun for Ted in being around us anymore, and he couldn't get a thing out of me, so he quit.

Dad stormed in on me and said it was all my fault. "I got you a tutor and what did you do?" he asked in the old, loud way. "You goofed off, and now he's quit. You haven't taken advantage of one advantage this place offers. You've hardly been into New York at all. I've had enough of your attitude. Bones's troubles are about solved and there's no reason to stay here. We're going back to Palm Beach."

That didn't bother me. Nor Sally. "I've been packed for a week," she told me. "There's no business left, anyhow. They found the rest of the money—in another bank—and cleared Bones. Didn't I tell you that?"

Her manner toward me had changed, too. She was still polite and considerate, but turned off.

Ted came and said good-bye before he left. "I wish I had been able to do more for you," he said in a stiff way.

"You did all you could," I told him. There was no point in being funny with him. He was too far down.

Hans and Carmen were the only ones who cared that we were going. Carmen cried when she and Hans were alone with me, and she threw her arms around me. "Ox . . . Ox . . . we'll surely miss you so."

"Come on, Carmen," Hans said, but he was upset, too.

I told Carmen I'd never forget her breakfasts, and she cheered up.

On the last morning she made me a monster, and I was about halfway through it when Jack Taffle came in the back way, with his hat in his hand.

"I heard you was leaving," he said, "and I wanted to say good-bye."

"I should have come to see you," I said. "And before now."

"Oh, you wouldn't have wanted to come over," he said. "I know that. How's the head?"

"Fine." The stitches had been out for a long time, and I'd practically forgotten about it.

We talked for a little, and then Hans came in and had to be told why Jack was there.

"You and Ox were good friends now?" he asked Jack.

"Not friends," Jack said, "just acquaintances." You couldn't get ahead of him.

There was more of that and then Hans asked him if he was staying busy and Jack said yes, that they had a lot of work to do. "Been fixing a lot of fence. There's a place back in the woods—near here, the old gate—where it had really fallen apart. The supe said it didn't look like normal wear and tear at all, more like a herd of elephants had been tearing it up. I told him it was probably lightning."

He said it absolutely deadpan, but I suppose he knew. Well, he almost had to. Jack was very sensitive.

He and I shook hands then.

"All the best." He didn't use my name.

"Same to you, Jack."

"I'll give you an old toast—'To the best that's yet to come.' That's what's waiting for all of us, whether we believe it or not." His calm eyes didn't show a thing while he was saying it.

The limousine was waiting, and we had one of those farewell scenes in front. Carmen cried some more and Hans shook hands all around. In the light, their uniforms were shabbier and dirtier than ever. Winston

Lochmann said he'd be coming to Palm Beach soon. Bones Blossom tried to get Hans to say dragon one more time, but it didn't work. There were other people there from the parties, and they were saying good-bye, too. It wasn't cold—just damp and heavy. It had been that way a lot since Christmas.

The three of us—Dad and Sally and I—had put on sort of a good face through the farewells, but when the car pulled off we went back to the way we were, not talking much and staying away from each other. It was the same on the plane going down.

26

AS LUCK WOULD HAVE IT, Mom had pulled
in the day before we did. If we'd come back a couple of
days earlier, she wouldn't have been there, and we could
have gotten settled in.

But she was there and waiting.

We dropped Sally at the Bracken place. She kissed
Dad lightly and said, "Take care, Barry."

"I'll call," Dad said, but you could tell he didn't have
his heart in it.

"You do that," she said. "Bye, Ox." She kissed me,
too, on the cheek, and kept her face turned away.

The first thing Mom said when we walked in was,
"Where's Sally?"

And Dad said, "Sally who?" It was a dumb thing to
say, but it was a dumb situation, and hard to resist doing
it that way.

Anyhow, that blew Mom, and she hit the roof. "Sally
Bracken, that's who! And I know she was with you on
Long Island all winter, and don't try to deny it, and all
this FRAAN stuff was only a cover," and so on.

Dad didn't fight it or deny it at all. He just poured

himself a big drink and went out to the pool house. She followed him, giving him the works all the way.

After a while I couldn't hear them.

I had to go back into regular school then, but it was sort of a relief to be back with ordinary kids. Ordinary rich kids, I should say. And it wasn't bad being back in warm weather.

The quarrel between Dad and Mom simmered down after a while, and they went back into what the people who write about wars call an armed truce.

Mom told me over and over how awful Argentina was, and asked me if Long Island was any good. I told her it wasn't.

Dale Tifton blew into town for a couple of weeks in March and we had a pretty good time. He told me some stories of what he'd been doing that I could hardly believe. Dale will do anything and he never cares afterward. He asked me what I'd been doing, and I told him I'd had to spend a few months around New York with Dad.

"There's a lot of action there if you know where to look," he said.

"I wouldn't know," I said.

"You let everything pass you by," he said, shaking his head. "I'm going to have to take you in hand."

Sally and Mom got to be friends again, and Mom says Sally has her eye on a new husband. Mom thinks that's all right—even funny—as long as it's not hers.

Sally came over one day last week when Mom was out and I saw her from the hall mixing herself a drink at the bar.

I said hello and she said, "Come on in here for a minute."

She'd been drinking, and her voice was husky and her eyes were filmy.

"Your mother's out," she said. "I didn't know. Thought I'd have a drink before I . . . leave."

I didn't say anything.

"Ox . . ." she began. And then she stopped, as though she'd forgotten what she wanted to say, or couldn't say it.

Then she did say, "Life's full of surprises."

I don't know whether it was what she meant to say at first, or whether it was something she said to cover forgetting, or to cover what she couldn't say.

She didn't say anything more, and we were standing there looking at each other. It was so still you could hear the ship's clock ticking behind the bar. Her hands were trembling very slightly—her glass wasn't quite steady—and her face looked ready to go.

She was pathetic, but she was all right, too.

"Yes, it is," I said finally, because I had to get away. "And there's nothing we can do about them."

I left her then. It seemed there should have been something else I could have done, or said, but there wasn't. All I could have done was be unhappy with her, and I didn't feel that way.

On the way upstairs, I decided I'd give Dale a ring.

He wasn't in much, but he was then. "I might take you up on getting out of here for a while," I told him. "Let's go this summer."

"That's too far off," he said.

"Only six weeks."

"I'm going to Barbados next week, and so I don't want to be going back to that part of the world. How about California?" he asked.

"No, everyone goes to California. Somewhere else, where no one goes."

"Mississippi?"

"We could start in that direction."

"Well . . ."

"You're the one who was talking about going some-place," I told him. "If you want to change your mind, or have too many other engagements, forget it. I'll go alone."

"Don't be so touchy," he said. "You know I'd rather bum around with you than with any of those beautiful older women who keep propositioning me. I always know what's going to happen with them, but with you—who knows what we'll get into?"

"All right." Once Dale says he'll do something, you know you can count on him.

"But, Ox . . . why do you want to bum around with me?"

"I figure you know the best places to eat."

"That's not it," he said. "But maybe you'll tell me someday."

"Maybe."

"And maybe not."

"And maybe not," I agreed. "Have a good time in Barbados."

"Never have."

"Your luck might change."

"That's right," he said. "Anyhow, it sounds right. You're a master of the cliché, Ox."

"I try."

"You succeed. You're in front all the way."

"Glad to hear that."

"Just don't let it go to your head."

"See you in June."

"I could say, 'Not if I see you first, but we're getting too old for that."

"Much too old."

"See you in June, old Ox," he said, and we hung up.

About the Author

JOHN NEY was born in St. Paul, Minnesota, and raised in New York and St. Louis. He has lived in England, Italy, Spain, Switzerland, and Austria, as well as in Palm Beach and on Long Island. A professional writer for more than twenty years, he has written novels, nonfiction books, and movie scripts. His previous novels about Ox Olmstead, *Ox: The Story of a Kid at the Top* and *Ox Goes North*, are considered two of the best books published for young people within the past five years.